MY EXORCISM KILLED ME

THE SENSITIVES BOOK TWO

RICK WOOD

BLOOD SPLATTER PRESS

RICK WOOD

Rick Wood is a British writer born in Cheltenham.

His love for writing came at an early age, as did his battle with mental health. After defeating his demons, he grew up and became a stand-up comedian, then a drama and English teacher, before giving it all up to become a full-time author.

He now lives in Loughborough, where he divides his time between watching horror, reading horror, and writing horror.

ALSO BY RICK WOOD

The Sensitives
The Sensitives
My Exorcism Killed Me
Close to Death
Demon's Daughter
Questions for the Devil
Repent
The Resurgence
Until the End

Blood Splatter Books
Psycho B*tches
Shutter House
This Book is Full of Bodies
Home Invasion

Cia Rose
After the Devil Has Won
After the End Has Begun
After the Living Have Lost
After the Dead Have Decayed

The Edward King Series
I Have the Sight
Descendant of Hell
An Exorcist Possessed
Blood of Hope
The World Ends Tonight

Anthologies
Twelve Days of Christmas Horror
Twelve Days of Christmas Horror Volume 2
Roses Are Red So Is Your Blood

Standalones
When Liberty Dies
The Death Club

Sean Mallon
The Art of Murder
Redemption of the Hopeless

Chronicles of the Infected
Zombie Attack
Zombie Defence
Zombie World

Non-Fiction
How to Write an Awesome Novel
The Writer's Room

Rick also publishes thrillers under the pseudonym Ed Grace...

Jay Sullivan

Assassin Down

Kill Them Quickly

The Bars That Hold Me

A Deadly Weapon

For Frank and Jack.

Both lovers of the classics, and classics themselves.

THEN

Wiltshire, England

A WHIRLWIND OF CHAOS ENCOMPASSED THE ROOM WITH SAVAGE intensity.

Fragments of glass.

Rough edges of wrecked pieces of wooden furniture.

Torn paper. Ripped clothes. Shattered light bulbs.

All discarded through the air with no consideration of the disorder it created.

There was nowhere you could step without stabbing a foot or pricking a finger. What had been an ordinary bedroom was now a mess of broken items. Some items lay still and unattended. Some items flapped on the floor like a dying fish. Most items clashed in the air in a hurricane of anarchy.

Derek Lansdale gripped his cross, securing his rigid fingers tightly around its base. He held it out firmly. Pointed it downwards at the helpless girl beneath him.

This hadn't been his toughest exorcism.

This hadn't even been his toughest night.

He had once endured war; but that was a long time ago. The rise of The Sensitives had changed things. Hell had struggled to pose a threat that Derek would deem substantial.

That considered, he still could not underplay how tough this exorcism had been. He had been at it for days, and was running on very little sleep. His aching muscles were growing weary and his head pounded with a fierce migraine.

He was mentally drained. But he had been here plenty of times before.

He had his young apprentice at his side – a Sensitive with an extraordinary power to banish demons from their victims. His wasn't the strongest power he'd ever witnessed, but what he lacked in ability, he made up for in passion.

His name was Julian Barth.

"Julian, I need your help!" Derek bellowed above the crashes and smashes of the room. A chair flew into the far wall, exploding into sharp shards of wood that blasted back into the room, causing Derek to duck.

Julian glanced to the only other people besides him, Derek and the girl, both of whom looked petrified.

One was a priest and the other, a doctor.

The priest, Derek had understood; but the doctor, Derek had raged about for days. This wasn't something he used to have to put up with, but with the church growing more and more concerned about society's lack of understanding toward what occurred during his exorcisms, it was now required. Following a few injuries, the Church had requested a higher level of risk management. Exorcism was yet to successfully merge with modern times.

Julian stood forward, his arms shaking, his lip quivering. This was his first. Derek had told him it would be tough, had forewarned him as to what he would witness. But Julian had expected a few shaking pieces of furniture, a few floating objects – not this. Not a scene of frenzied, torturous mania.

Julian took Derek's side, looking upon the vulnerable girl helplessly restrained to the bed.

Her face was that of Anna Bennett. She was an innocent,

playful, yet shy twelve-year-old girl. She worked hard at school, picked flowers for her teachers, and was always polite to everyone she met.

Except, what they were looking at was not Anna.

In body, yes. It was Anna's skin. Her fingers, her toes. But not her eyes.

It was in her eyes that you couldn't escape an undeniable presence of evil.

It was in her cracked lips, stained skin, and writhing body that the demon lived, causing the girl constant, excruciating agony.

Blood soaked from her crotch, mixing with the urine stains on the bed sheets. Julian had been rendered speechless upon first meeting Anna and witnessing the morbid fascination the demon had with focussing its violent attacks on her crotch. It was a second between her innocent smile and her dinner fork being thrust inside of herself.

"Julian, damn it, I need you to focus!" Derek demanded.

Julian realised he had been in a daydream, thinking about his hesitance, his trepidation, to the point that he had ended up neglecting his responsibilities.

"What do you want me to do, Derek?" he asked, flinching at the fragile wobble of his voice.

"Where is your cross, boy?"

Julian raised his hand, holding his cross out.

"Hold it firmly, like you bloody-well mean it!" Derek prompted.

Julian grasped the cross, pointing it at the demon with forced, disingenuous confidence.

"Now repeat after me. Be gone, demon!"

"Be gone, demon."

"Louder! *Be gone, demon!*"

"Be gone, demon!"

Anna's mouth opened, black saliva trickling down her chin,

and she projectile vomited bloody lumps that splashed down her legs and the bed sheets, flicking onto Julian's shoes.

"Er, Mr Lansdale," came a shy voice from the doctor behind. "I'm concerned."

"About what?" snapped Derek. He'd done enough of these rituals without doctors; he wasn't particularly open to listening to what they had to say just because the Church wanted to afford their exorcists more protection.

Protection from what? The law?

There were far harsher things out there worth protecting themselves from.

"That's the fifth time she's been sick. I'm worried she may not be hydrated. When was the last time you allowed her a glass of water?"

A glass of water?

Derek turned his bemused face to the doctor, full of disdain for his ridiculous contribution.

"Shut up, you stuffy old man," Derek replied, then realised how hypocritical his words were; he was hardly the spritely, energetic young man he used to be.

"You're hurting me..." came an innocent young girl's voice from the face of the wretched demon. It was playing on the doctor's insecurities, but the doctor would not have the experience that Derek had that allowed him to identify the demon's tactics.

"Ignore it," Derek told Julian, ignoring the doctor. "It will imitate the host, try to get a rise from us."

"I need water... I need food... Please..."

"Derek," Julian offered, concerned about the girl's wellbeing.

"Enough!" Derek interrupted, full of irritation. "You need to learn to be tough. A demon will exploit any weakness. Show it nothing but strength."

Julian nodded obediently.

"Behold the cross of the Lord; flee bands of enemies," Derek continued, spitting his prayer with utter detest. "May thy mercy, Lord, descend upon us. Be gone, demon!"

Julian could only watch as the demon stopped writhing and grew still, collapsing into a heap.

Every object in the room that had been firing around in circles fell to the floor with a heavy thud. Furniture, glass, torn clothes – everything came hurtling down to the surface.

A calm tranquility descended upon the room. Like the morning after a heavy night.

At first, they thought the exorcism had been successful.

With decades of experience working against him, Derek was tempted to believe that this was a success also. But he knew enough to know that this may just have been the eye of the storm.

Derek fell against the wall, slumping to the floor, breathing quickly, panting, relishing the opportunity for a break. The older he got, the tougher this became. He could feel his bones growing weaker, his muscles stiff, and his body removed of energy.

Julian was the next generation now. Derek needed to be able to pass his knowledge along and retire. Somewhere in the country, maybe. A nice cottage with a view.

Julian didn't rest. There was something about Anna's state that desperately concerned him.

He took a few cautious steps toward the girl. The closer he tiptoed forward, the more his mind filled with dread.

It all went into slow motion. He reached the girl's side, watching her lying motionless. Her eyes were wide open, but they didn't move. Her chest didn't rise.

He placed two fingers on the side of her neck.

He couldn't feel a pulse.

"Doctor!" Julian exclaimed, turning toward the doctor, who came rushing forward.

The doctor felt for the girl's pulse, then turned back to Derek with terror.

"What?" Derek asked, standing, growing uneasy. "What is it?"

The doctor dragged the girl from the bed and onto the floor, ensuring she was on a hard surface. Without hesitation, he began CPR. He pushed down on the girl's chest repeatedly, doing all he could to restart her heart. He sucked up air and breathed out into her mouth, multiple times, again and again, persisting.

Julian stood next to Derek for what felt like an age, shaking his head, his eyes fighting back tears. He didn't want to look weak in front of Derek.

He looked at Derek's face, looking to see if this was normal, looking for an indication as to how Julian should be acting.

Derek's wide eyes continued to stare at the helpless body of the girl lying on the floor. A flicker of vulnerability passed over his face, but he did his best to conceal it.

This was going to change everything, and he knew it.

"I got cocky," Derek whispered to himself.

No one responded. No one answered. No one confirmed that he had or he hadn't. Everyone just stared.

Stared at the doctor persevering in his attempt to save the girl's life.

Eventually, the doctor stopped. Out of breath, his head turned. Slowly. Looking over the faces waiting for his conclusion.

The doctor just stared at the wide eyes gazing back at him.

"Well?" Julian prompted.

"She's..." the doctor began, pausing, unable to find the words. "She's... dead."

Derek fell to his knees.

Julian watched as Derek shook his head, again and again, rapidly twisting back and forth in denial.

"No..." Derek muttered. "No, no, no, no..."

Julian backed up, covering his face, closing his eyes, bowing his head. He tried looking elsewhere. Away from the girl, away from Derek, endeavouring to find a point in the room he could look where he wouldn't be having to face what had just happened.

What would their excuse to the authorities be?

A demon possessed her?

They would lock them away in a padded cell.

And the girl...

Her mother was waiting downstairs, full of worry, expecting them to have the solution. To rid the horrid entity from her daughter's body.

Soon, they would have to go downstairs and give her the news. Deliver the awful news of her daughter's death.

The mother had been so hopeful. Derek had told her, "No demon has beaten me yet."

She had thought that Derek was her saviour.

And now...

Julian wanted to punch something. To turn the furniture upside down, to kick a chair across the room, to smash a window.

But he didn't.

He didn't even move.

He couldn't.

He just stared absently at the corpse lying on the bed in its own urine, sick, and blood.

NOW

4 years later

Tewkesbury, Gloucestershire

2

JULIAN'S HEAVY SLEEP ENDED ABRUPTLY AS HE BOLTED UPRIGHT like a plank.

For a few minutes he sat. Still. Panting and sweating as his awareness gradually readjusted. His body remained motionless but for his chest, which rapidly expanded and retracted with the heaviness of his breathing.

He tried to prop himself up, but his arms wobbled, as unsteady as his mind. He endeavoured to push himself to a state of balance, but his elbows continued to give way.

That dream.

Again.

That same damn dream.

Anna dies like she does every night.

Her face looks back at him. Her eyes held wide open as if pulled apart by pins. Her pupils fixed on his, full of horror yet absent of life. Chills run down his spine. He is left rooted to the spot in terror.

His mouth won't form words.

His mind won't form thoughts.

It was the same face he saw in every victim of demonic possession he helped. Any time he started the first prayer of an exorcism. Any time he held that cross in his trembling hands and recited that same prayer.

Sure, it was another person, and another helpless soul he was determined to help. But, whenever he looked into their eyes – as in, really looked into their eyes – it was Anna, all over again.

The night fogged his room with darkness. Yet, in his dreams, he saw her as clear as day. What had been the life of an enthusiastic, bubbly twelve-year-old morphed into the stiffened face of a corpse revealing the onset of rigor mortis.

His breath calmed. It was still furious, with a pace to his panting that almost suffocated him, but he was gradually regaining control. As he took that control and allowed his breathing to slow, to continue to calm, his mind finally reached the point where he could focus his blurry vision on the shadows around him.

He was topless. Sweating profusely on a cold autumn night.

The clock read 3.40 a.m.

The same hour.

No need to explain why. Derek had taught him about the witching hour, and what it was.

It was the hour of the demonic. The hour when hell was at its strongest, and committing the foulest acts.

But Julian did not believe it was hell that was haunting him. He believed it was himself. And he would not allow himself to let his mind dwell on other possibilities, just because of the things he had seen.

He hung his head. He felt weak. He needed help.

"Derek..." he whispered, unsure why. The word came out as cold breath that lingered in a haze before him, then protruded into vague smoke.

He rotated his body and placed his bare feet on the carpet. He buried his head in his hands, running his fingers through his soaking hair, sticky with perspiration.

Anna.

She was still there, imprinted on the forefront of his mind. Her cold, dead face, still haunting him.

He wondered if it still haunted Derek.

He switched on a lamp light and grimaced at its brightness, squinting as his eyes adapted to its mild luminosity. He picked up his phone, scrolled through his address book, then put it to his ear.

Waited a few moments.

"Hello?" came a voice at the end.

"Hi, I would like to speak to Derek Lansdale, please."

"Do you know what time this is?" came the irritated voice at the other end of the phone.

"Erm... yeah, I do. Is it possible for me to speak to him?"

"No!" replied the ill-tempered recipient of his late call. "You can call during normal hours like everyone else."

The line went dead.

The one man he counted on. Unable to talk.

It wasn't fair. Derek didn't deserve the fate he had been bestowed. The predicament he was in for trying to help a young girl.

Julian closed his eyes. Considered trying to fall back to sleep, but knew he would not be successful. The constant reoccurrence of these late-night awakenings was making him sluggish in the day, but now he felt wide awake.

His dried sweat was growing cold as it stuck to his skin in the cool night air and he slid a loose t-shirt over his chest. He left his room and trudged across his flat to the kitchen. He opened the fridge, took out a pint of milk, and poured himself a glass.

13

He leant against the side, absentmindedly sipping, his mind elsewhere. His mind still with Derek. With Anna.

He had to get himself together.

He could never let April see him like this. Or Oscar. No one could see his weaknesses. He was meant to lead them, meant to guide them. Not burden them.

Derek was the only one who could see this side of him. Except, Derek couldn't be there for him anymore. Not like he used to be.

He gulped down the rest of his milk, placed the glass in the sink, and walked back to his room.

He froze.

A whisper carried across the room, as if coming from outside, sailing across the shuffle of the night air. It was a windy night, and he was sure it was just his tired mind forming patterns out of sounds. Chances are, what he thought he heard was just the wind beating against branches or soaring through the cracks of the windows.

Still, it sounded specific.

It sounded as if someone had whispered his name.

He shook his head to himself.

He was a paranormal investigator. He knew what constituted paranoia and what constituted genuine supernatural phenomena.

"Julian…" it whispered once more, ever so faintly, with the rustle of a tree branch tapping against the window.

It was the weather.

Grow up.

He had no inkling or awareness of a feeling of the supernatural in his flat. It was just his tired sub-conscious haunting him. Not a ghost. He was a strong, experienced Sensitive – he would know.

Still.

It was odd.

Shaking his head to himself, he returned to his bedroom and opened a political thriller on his Kindle, trying to keep his mind away from thoughts of demons and ghosts.

He read until he fell back to sleep.

3

Oscar absently stirred his coffee, staring at the milk mixing with the water.

"You know you're meant to drink coffee, right? Not just stir it," teased April, smirking playfully as she sipped her hot chocolate.

Oscar took a big, deep breath, got ready to speak, found the words, urged them to his mouth, and...

"Yeah," was all he could muster.

You absolute wuss. You complete and utter loser. Get a grip! You've battled demons, and you can't even tell a girl how you feel!

It was the ninth time he and April had been together like this. In a situation, alone, with intimate conversation. It was another occasion that left Oscar racking his mind with the question: *is this a date?*

It felt like a date. It was just those two, no Julian. Alone. Together. Talking and smiling at each other. Getting dressed up.

Only for it to amount to nothing.

Oscar was pretty sure he was close to being friend-zoned now, if he hadn't been already.

He should have gone in for the kiss on that first date. Looking back, it was obvious. She'd held his eye contact, fiddled with her keys at the door, then, at the last minute, his belly had filled with a swarm of butterflies. He overthought it, and he backed out.

Now, here they were. Alone. Again. Together. He was wearing a shirt.

He never wore shirts.

Surely, she knew from his shirt that this was a serious occasion?

Or, maybe she's normal, and she doesn't pay attention to everything I wear and keep track of how I attribute the formality of my clothes relative to the occasion.

He could have shown up in a tuxedo, top hat, and tails, and she would have had no idea.

"So..." Oscar began, trying not to let the silence last too long. If it lasted too long, then she would decide she felt uncomfortable with him, decide she no longer liked him, and it wasn't going to happen – that is, if she had actually liked him in the first place.

Here I go, overthinking it again.

"So...?" April repeated, awaiting the thought Oscar was readying himself to verbalise.

"So... how long have we known each other?"

April let out a sigh, thinking carefully before returning her beautiful hazel eyes back to Oscar's reddening face.

"Nine months?" April asked.

She was close.

It's actually eight months, twenty-three days, four hours, and around fifteen minutes.

"Yeah, nine months, something like that," Oscar confirmed. "See, over that time..."

Oscar went to speak, then found his tongue twisting into a fattened obstruction. Her purple hair was tied into a long ponytail beneath a red bandana, and flung loosely over her shoulder. She had a spiky collar on, flared jeans, and a hoodie from some band Oscar had never heard of, with her sleeves pulled up enough to reveal her funky Tim Burton tattoos and multiple music festival bracelets.

"Over that time... what?" April replied, raising her eyebrows and sticking out her bottom lip, as if waiting for Oscar to finish that sentence.

"Well..." Oscar attempted to resume. "We've fought a lot of demons. A lot of ghosts."

"A few."

Sixteen demons, three poltergeists, one banshee, two frauds, and eight seances.

"Yeah, a few."

Oscar took a large sip of his coffee, found that it was too hot and it scalded his tongue, yet held it painfully in his mouth. He paused, not wanting to swallow and burn his throat, but not wanting to spit it back out into his cup in front of April.

April grew confused, watching him in limbo, halted, with the liquid held behind his lips.

"Are you okay?" she asked, stifling a giggle at his expense.

"Mmhm," he lied.

I'm going to have to swallow. It's the only way.

He closed his eyes, readied himself, and gulped down the hot liquid that stung the back of his throat. He attempted to conceal his pain, wincing and flinching in restraint.

"You're an odd creature," April spiritedly observed.

An odd creature?

Is that a good thing? Should I say thank you? Does that mean she likes me? Is odd good? Is being a creature good? Is any of this good?

"Er... cheers."

"You're welcome," April chuckled, taking a sip of her hot chocolate that she seemed to manage to drink without worrying about it burning her whatsoever.

18

"So, we've known each other long enough to be, like, good friends, yeah?"

April appeared bemused. "...Yeah."

"Good. Good."

This was it.

Come on, Oscar.

Suck it up.

It's time.

"Well, in that time, I've grown quite fond of you," he blurted out, on a roll, not about to stop. "And I actually really quite like–"

April's phone blared out, interrupting Oscar dead in his tracks.

She picked it up and looked at it.

"Sorry, it's Julian," she spoke, then read her text.

Bloody Julian. That sodding guy. I was about to say it...

"Oh my God!" April exclaimed as she read her message, her eyebrows raised. "Jeeze. I can't believe this."

"What? What is it?"

April leant toward Oscar.

"He says it's time for you to meet Derek."

4

Detective Inspector Jason Lyle strode into the hospital, stroking his trimmed beard with one hand as the other nestled comfortably in his pocket. He was used to unusual crime scenes, and he had been told that this was no exception.

"So, what have we got?" he demanded of his colleague.

"We have a body, and… well… you'd better come see."

Jason followed the officer up the stairs until they reached the children's ward on the fourth floor.

He glanced at the sick children in the beds as he paced past, feeling a sense of morbidity. Pale children weakly prodding at hospital food, attached to machines barely keeping them alive. It made him picture his child in that position and considered how devastating an experience that would be.

No wonder someone snapped in this place if tragically ill children surround them every day.

As they approached the office of the deceased doctor, he paused beside the door and signed in. After stepping into his white suit, he stepped inside.

The body of a middle-aged man lay on the floor. His wide eyes were still open, and his hands were stuck rigidly upwards with his fingers spread out. He looked like he died stuck in a state of shock. Rigor mortis held him rigidly in place, but how? It would have taken at least two hours to set in – so how had his body remained in this position following death, instead of collapsing on the floor?

Jason instantly understood why he had been called. No one could answer this question, and that was why they had resorted to phoning him. He had grown a distinct reputation as a detective with a penchant for unusual cases.

"Talk me through it," he instructed his colleague.

"Well, if you have a look at the lacerations on his throat, there are marks against his oesophagus, showing that he was clearly strangled. And he is stuck in a position of shock, which is puzzling, to say the least. But that's not the strange part."

"Well, what is the strange part?" Jason replied, growing impatient.

"He was shown to have been strangled to death, but the way that he is propped, he – he was petrified in his final moments. He saw something that stuck him like this. It totally contrasts with the notion of a slow death from strangulation, compared to a death of sudden shock, and – well, he appears to have died from both. It's just, well, how is that possible when both take such a vastly different amount of time to kill a guy?"

Jason crouched beside the body, scrutinising it with his searching eyes.

True, the victim had been strangled to death. Something that could easily have taken ten minutes.

Yet it was also true that the victim appeared to have been shocked to death within seconds.

The victim must have seen something. Something when he was close to death, something that terrified him.

But what?

"There's more," Jason's colleague told him.

"More?"

"We've already run DNA. There's no one's DNA on his throat but his. It's as if no one else was in here with him. Similarly, there are no footprints to the door that we can find with either UV or forensic testing. There's no sign of a break-in on the windows. It's as if he did it to himself."

"That's not possible."

"Absolutely, it's not possible. You can't asphyxiate yourself; you'd pass out and relieve the pressure before you could finish. But he absolutely finished."

"Curious."

Jason knew why his scatterbrained subordinate couldn't figure out what had happened.

Because he hadn't seen the things Jason had.

He hadn't witnessed what Jason had witnessed.

This was another case that went down as 'not of this world.' It was not one that would be solved with ordinary methods.

Luckily, Jason knew exactly whom to talk to.

5

OSCAR FIDGETED NERVOUSLY IN THE BACKSEAT, GAZING AT THE fields darting quickly past the window.

Wherever Derek lived, it appeared to be in the middle of nowhere. Oscar wasn't sure if he'd seen an actual building for miles.

Maybe he's one of those crazy old men who live in the middle of nowhere, but are geniuses despite being so crazy...

He concluded that he'd watched too many movies, and willed himself to think rationally. He knew very little about Derek, just that he was a war hero. What war, exactly, Oscar wasn't sure.

But from the way Julian spoke about him with such admiration, Oscar knew he must be a great man. It took a lot for Julian to pay someone a compliment, never mind place them on the pedestal he had so done with Derek.

"So, who is Derek, exactly?" Oscar blurted out, then wished he'd thought of a more tactful way to ask the question.

April looked to Julian beside her in the driver's seat. The way Julian's eyes lit up when he spoke about Derek always made her smile.

"Imagine we are all children of the paranormal," Julian answered philosophically. "He would be the father."

"I don't understand. You said he fought in wars?"

"I did. He fought in a war you will never know about because the Church is very good at covering it up. Even if it did involve demons climbing out of the pit of hell and angels coming down from the sky."

Oscar raised his eyebrows and lifted his nose. Church cover-up? Demons climbing out of hell? Angels?

It all seemed a bit far-fetched.

"I don't think you could ever believe how far our battle against hell went until you go to the depths Derek has," Julian spoke ardently, irritated about the scepticism toward his mentor. "This entire world would be non-existent if it weren't for him."

"What exactly did Derek do in this war?"

"He performed an exorcism on the antichrist. At one point, he even faced the devil itself."

Oscar raised his eyebrows in astonishment. He had witnessed exorcisms on children and teenagers that took vast amounts of energy and respite. To actually perform it on an heir to the devil's throne...

Derek Lansdale must have some incredible stories.

"Don't ask him about it," Julian told Oscar, as if reading his mind.

"What?" Oscar retorted. "Why not?"

"You can never comprehend the sacrifices Derek had to make in that war. It took a lot out of him."

I bet.

Oscar understood. It sounded like Derek had been through a lot, and maybe he wouldn't want to talk about it if he'd had to endure such arduous trials. Such things rarely came without sacrifice.

The thought of this only made his nerves worse. He had

seen a lot in his short stint as a paranormal investigator. Still, compared to Julian and April, his experience was small; but compared to Derek, his experience was tiny.

His hands fidgeted, his stomach fluttered, his knees shook. His eyes darted back and forth, not knowing where to look.

"Calm down," came April's ever-soothing voice. Oscar noticed her glancing at him in the mirror. "You can't go in to face a man like this in that state."

"In what state?" Oscar asked, trying to keep his leg still and his hands non-fidgety.

"I know you well enough by now, Oscar," April replied play-fully, "to know when you are nervous and overthinking. Just be cool."

'Just be cool.'

Pah!

Easy for April to say, she *was* cool. If Oscar tried to pull off purple hair or Tim Burton tattoos he'd look like a dork. She pulled them off with ease. She was the epitome of cool. Oscar was the epitome of...

I don't know if I really want to finish that sentence.

He looked out the window, watching more fields go by. The road transformed into a one-lane country road, but Julian didn't have to stop too many times for other cars to get past.

"Jeeze, he must live in the middle of nowhere," Oscar declared, then noted Julian's knowing grin in the mirror.

"Yes." Julian nodded cockily. "He does."

Oscar grew confused. Why was Julian being so ominous? Where were they going? Under a bridge? A magical hut? *South bloody Africa?*

"So where exactly does he live?"

"You'll see now, we're here."

They entered a car park, where Julian stopped the car.

Oscar stood out of the car, looking at the building before him with dropped jaw.

Of all the places they were going to end up, this was the last place Oscar had expected.

He glanced at Julian, who nodded confirmation that they were at the right place, then turned his gaze to the exterior of Gloucester Prison.

6

A PRISON.

Of all the places Oscar had expected to end up, this was bottom of the list.

He was a mess of nerves and apprehension. He'd never even considered what it would be like to enter a prison before.

He looked to Julian to see how to behave, and felt a brief sting of resentment for how cool and together he appeared. He wondered if Julian had felt like he did the first time he entered the prison – awkward and anxious.

He looked to April instead, desperate for some indication of how to act. As far as Oscar was aware, April had been here once a few months ago, and this was her second time. Yet she still seemed to walk the path with gumption and confidence, without an ounce of trepidation.

Oscar knew her better than that.

Her face was steely, resolute. It was a stony, expressionless piece of art; it was the face of someone forcing themselves to portray no anxiety.

But why should they feel anxiety? They were entering as visitors, not as prisoners. Oscar had nothing to worry about.

Oscar imagined how he would fare in prison. He'd likely be beaten up by some butch murderous inmate boasting about their victims, before going back to his cell and having to deal with the stench of the commode after his hostile cellmate had used it.

I would not survive in a prison.

They approached a large, dark-blue door with a semicircle atop covered with square bars. It was surrounded by cream bricks, large slabs of stone separating the inside from the out.

Julian opened the door and went into a room where he had a brief conversation with someone Oscar couldn't see. Moments later, a prison officer walked out, waving them to follow. It struck Oscar how the prison officer had nothing to protect himself with; just a chain with keys attached, a white shirt with black locks on the shoulders and smart black trousers. Then again, it made sense – if officers were to carry a weapon there was a chance that a prisoner could take it.

Oscar had once heard a statistic that ninety percent of prison inmates have a weapon on them at any time; which made him even more terrified to be setting foot inside.

"Wait here," the prison officer instructed with a thick Scottish accent. The man walked over to a female prison officer, who approached April.

Oscar watched as the male and female officers searched Julian and April respectively. He watched with bemusement as he wondered how a female prison officer would survive in a male prison, then wondered if it was sexist for him to think that.

Once they had finished, the man stood before Oscar, looking at him expectantly.

"Hi," Oscar offered.

"Open your mouth," the prison officer instructed with a face like lead.

Feeling a little stupid for his weak, sensitive *hi*, and

knowing that Julian was stood with his hand on his hips and rolling his eyes, Oscar reluctantly opened his mouth. The officer searched under his tongue with something that felt like prickly cardboard.

"Open your arms."

Oscar did as he was told and waited as the man patted him down with excruciating thoroughness, searching every pocket, and feeling every inch of his legs.

"Your shoes."

Oscar looked back blankly, then abruptly realised that he was meant to take them off. He removed his daps, giving them to the prison officer and feeling slightly bad for how stinky they must smell. He watched as they were inspected, then returned them to his feet.

"This way," the officer told Julian, who followed him to another room. April followed also, prompting Oscar to suddenly wake up and trail behind them. Oscar, still in the middle of fastening his laces, finished a double knot and stumbled after them.

He looked down as he walked over a circular print on the marble floor that read *H.M. Prison Gloucester*, with a picture of gates with two keys over the top and chains on the side.

Wonder why they bother with art on a prison floor...

Oscar followed the others, running slightly to keep up, as they were taken through a few twisting corridors with cream-coloured walls and dark-blue bars.

Strange, Oscar had always imagined prison bars to be grey and rusty, whereas these appeared fresh, with only occasional cracks in the paint.

They were led to a large hall. In the far corner was a tuck shop, next to a children's play area. Throughout the hall were circular tables screwed to the ground, with four chairs around each, also fastened to the floor.

Various families sat waiting. Oscar was surprised at the

appearance of these families. They all seemed so... normal. Children were well-kept and tidy, women were well-groomed, and men looked soft and friendly.

It struck Oscar how many generalisations and assumptions he had carried with him that were naïvely untrue.

They were directed to a table, where they sat and waited. Over the course of fifteen to twenty minutes, various prisoners came through, each being finger printed and given a bib they were made to wear as they entered. Emotions ran high as they greeted their families and friends.

It made Oscar wonder how he was supposed to act when he met Derek.

Then, as if answering his question, April and Julian suddenly rose. Oscar joined in, wanting to be respectful to the man he was about to meet. He had seen a picture of this man in Julian's home, with a much younger-looking Julian. Derek had been dressed impeccably in a suit, a neatly trimmed beard, and parted grey hair. He had looked like a university professor would stereotypically look – smart, friendly, and approachable. The picture had presented Derek Lansdale as someone wizened with age and experience.

But when Oscar saw the man approaching, he saw nothing of the man in the picture, and he was instantly taken aback. As Derek smiled weakly at Julian, Oscar did his best to conceal his shock.

The man was unhealthily thin; Oscar could practically see ribs through the guy's t-shirt. His beard was long and unkempt, and he hobbled forward, leaning over a walking stick he relied heavily upon. It took an age for him to approach, and as he did, his bony facial features turned into delight. Oscar had initially guessed that this man was in his fifties, but he looked far older and bedraggled.

"Julian," Derek warmly greeted, an aged weakness in his voice. "It is so good to see you."

"And you, Derek." Julian took Derek's hand and held it in both of his, greeting him warmly. "You remember April."

"Of course," Derek answered, his grin spreading from cheek to cheek. "It is a delight to see you again, my dear."

"It's an honour," April answered, taking his hand in hers and shaking it firmly. Oscar wondered how firmly he was going to be able to shake Derek's hand without breaking him.

"And this is Oscar," Julian introduced.

Derek's face lit up. He looked overcome with joy, nodding vigorously, practically beaming.

"It is a privilege to meet you, my friend," Derek offered so kindly that Oscar wondered how on earth someone so caring could end up in prison.

"The privilege is mine," Oscar returned, feeling proud for not messing up his response. He took Derek's hand and shook it warmly, smiling back at him as politely as he could.

Derek backed into his seat slowly, using a hand on his walking stick to lower himself down.

"Oh, God, I forgot to get you anything from the tuck shop," Julian suddenly remembered, and it surprised Oscar to see Julian so flustered in someone else's presence, having been the one who always had it together. "Let me go get you something."

"Nonsense, nonsense." Derek waved Julian's concerns away with his hand. "Snacks would only distract me from meeting our marvellous new Sensitive."

Oscar blushed.

He's talking about me.

"Tell me about yourself, Oscar," Derek prompted in a slow but friendly manner. "Where do you come from?"

"I come from Tewkesbury, down the road."

"Ah, Tewkesbury. I've been there many a time. Have you been in the Olde Black Bull?"

"You mean that rackety old pub?"

31

"Oh, it's no rackety old pub, my friend. It is one of the most haunted buildings in the country."

Oscar stuck his bottom lip out. He didn't know that. He'd always assumed there could be nothing interesting about his hometown.

"And how are you finding your gift? April tells me you've been supremely helpful so far."

"Well, I hope I have," Oscar spoke, trying to remain focused and polite at all times, desperate not to come off as rude, impolite, or even worse – naïve. "It's been quite the experience so far."

"Oh, it will be. It will be."

A moment of awkward silence settled upon them, and Oscar racked his mind for something to say, finding himself craving Derek's approval.

"Derek," Julian interrupted. "I wondered if we might have a word in private."

"Of course, of course."

"We'll be right outside," April announced, and stood up.

Oscar was staring so gormlessly at Derek with eyes of fascination that he didn't realise it was his cue to leave, and ended up being prodded on the shoulder quite forcefully by April.

"It was lovely to see you again, April," Derek told her.

"It was lovely to see you too."

"And it was an honour to meet you, Oscar." Derek gave him a subtle wink that made Oscar fill with childlike excitement.

"You too," he answered, and followed April out of the room.

As they left, a prison officer met them to guide them to the exit.

"What a lovely man," Oscar spoke.

"Derek is the best," April confirmed as they were guided through the final exit doors and into the car park. "We owe him so much."

"What do you mean?"

"You really have no idea what Derek did for us, do you?"

She smiled knowingly as she unlocked the car, leaving Oscar desperately longing to know what she meant.

7

"HE SEEMS LIKE A NICE BOY," DEREK COMMENTED.

Julian shrugged.

"He's nice enough," Julian answered with a blase attitude. "But he seems more determined on getting into April's pants than he does the job."

"Give him time."

"Time? He's young, pathetic, and seems to not have a clue what he's doing."

"I remember someone who was like that once." Derek smiled and peered knowingly at Julian.

Julian forced a chuckle. Derek was right. Julian had been incredibly hormonal and arrogant when they had first met. Not to mention impatient. And innocent. And annoying.

Julian sighed a sigh of hesitation. He tapped his hands on the table a few times, let out a final huff, then turned to Derek, deciding to broach the subject.

"How have things been?" he asked.

"Fine," Derek answered, being purposefully obtuse.

"You know what I mean. Has anything else been going on in the prison?"

Derek looked over his shoulder. The nearest prison officer was wandering past a family a few tables away.

"Yes," Derek answered. "And no. Yes, the same things have been happening, and no, you needn't concern yourself."

"Derek–"

"I am perfectly capable of taking care of myself against whatever entity is in here," Derek insisted. "Don't you know who I am?"

Julian laughed. Only he could recognise the joke in Derek's question – the man was far too humble to ever really say anything like that.

Then Julian's laughter died, recognising Derek's throwaway question as a clear avoidance technique, and refused to let the subject go.

"You need my help, Derek. If there is something here, and it's harming prisoners, or *you*, then..."

Julian sighed despondently. How do you tell someone with Derek's vast experience that they need to let someone help them? Derek was not only a war hero, but he was a better man and a better mentor than Julian could ever put into words.

But he hobbled around with a walking stick! His muscles ached after a short walk. His mind was weary and tired and slow to respond – how was Julian meant to tell him that?

"Like I said, Julian. I am quite capable of fighting the demonic and the ghostly."

"Once, you were," Julian blurted out honestly. "A long time ago, you would have shown everyone how it's done. You would have put your Sensitives-in-training to shame; you would have put us in our place and proven that arrogance is our downfall. But not now."

"Why not now?"

"Because look at you, Derek. You're thin. You're weak. You tell me nothing's wrong, and I believe you, but..."

"Say it," Derek demanded.

Derek had always appreciated direct, blunt honesty, rather than what he called, "fannying about around the subject."

"You're old. You're not the man you once were."

"I'm fifty-four."

"Yes. You are fifty-four. And in those fifty-four years, you have done more than most people could hope to do in hundreds – and it has quite clearly worn you down."

Derek fell silent. Julian watched as he dropped his head in quiet contemplation, feeling a sudden pang of guilt. Derek had done so much for him...

Well then, maybe this was his way of repaying him! After all, life is just one big circle. You're born and you rely on others, then you grow up, then you grow old, and rely on others again. Derek just needed to realise...

No. Who am I to tell a man like Derek he needs help?

"I'm sorry, Derek, I–"

"Never apologise for something that you mean, otherwise you're being insincere."

Derek spoke without looking up. A few minutes of silence hung over the table like a black cloud. Julian did his best to think of something to say, but he knew that in this situation, it was best to let Derek find the first word.

"Yes, Julian, I get it," Derek reluctantly admitted. "But, as far as we are aware, this is not a demon, and probably just some petty poltergeist. Until we know anything more, I can still handle some little poltergeist."

"Time's up!" called out the prison officer.

Julian looked up. They were the last left in the room. Everyone else was gone.

That was odd. He didn't see them go.

"I keep having dreams," Julian softly revealed. "About..."

"About what?"

"About Anna."

Derek looked back at him with an eerie curiosity.

36

A prison officer appeared behind him. "Time to go."

Julian tried to gauge the look on Derek's face, but couldn't. It was as if Derek's expression had fallen into a cold lucidity. Deep thoughts burdening a heavy mind behind those ageing eyes – but what? What were those thoughts? What was he thinking?

Julian needed guidance. He needed Derek to say something.

"All the best, Julian," Derek finally spoke, before turning and being led away.

Julian was completely alone, left to sit amongst a room of unanswered questions.

THEN

8

AMAZEMENT OVERCAME JULIAN'S EYES, GROWING UPON HIM LIKE a sunrise. His energetic mind could hardly conceive of the information Derek was bestowing upon his youthful shoulders.

"A Sensitive?" Julian remarked. "Why the hell are they called Sensitives?"

"Not they, you," Derek pointed out, "are termed a Sensitive, and aptly so. It refers to how you have a sensitivity to the paranormal that others do not. You can see, feel, or even do things that others would not believe are real."

Julian looked around himself in astonishment. This guy had walked into his place of work, claimed to know who he was, then spent three weeks taking him on a whirlwind of education. He had since learnt what was truly possible in both this life, and beyond it. He'd seen things he hadn't dreamt of being able to see, and been taught things he would never have possibly thought true.

"Why, though?" Julian's inexperienced mind wondered. "Why am I a Sensitive? Why *me*?"

"Because heaven conceived *you*. There is something within

you, something you can use. We can't be entirely sure of what your gift is, but from what I've seen, I would imagine you to be a talented exorcist."

"An exorcist?"

Now Derek was having him on.

An exorcist?

Such a thing only exists in movies, and not the kind that Julian would normally watch. He had always found the whole concept too far-fetched, and avoided horrors. He was far more at home with an Academy-Award winning drama; far more realistic.

How little he knew.

"I am an accomplished exorcist myself," Derek humbly asserted. "And have banished many demons from the bodies of many victims."

"But how can you be sure it's a demon, and not just, you know, a nutter?"

Derek smirked. Julian was asking the right questions.

"Julian, I would be annoyed if you didn't ask me such a thing."

Julian smiled, chuffed to have been delivered a compliment by this man who seemed to have such vast life experience.

"We do rigorous testing to ensure the person involved is a victim, and not one with severe mental health issues," Derek told Julian. "And I'll be honest with you – ninety-nine percent of the time it proves to be the latter."

"So how do you know for sure?"

"Tell me, Julian – have you ever seen a mentally ill person levitate six feet high off a bed? Speak in Latin when they don't even know what Latin is? Have objects fly around the room of their own accord whenever you recite a prayer?"

"I guess not."

"Julian, I admire your gumption – I too was an atheist before I understood how things were. Which is good, so you should be – no proof, no belief, that's what I've always said." He knelt against the table and leant toward Julian. "Being honest, I'm not entirely sure if I am on board with the whole concept of God, even after what I've seen. But I know what I've seen. And I know what you will see too."

Julian was in awe, totally overcome with wonder. This man had shown him so many things, had opened his eyes to a whole world he didn't even know was possible.

Derek opened his bag and placed several objects upon the table.

"This is a cross, as I'm sure you recognise." Derek pointed to his first item. "Then these are rosary beads, this is holy water. These are essential items you need to defeat a demon in an exorcism."

Julian looked over the items with bemusement, then back to Derek.

"But, Derek, how do you defeat something as powerful as a demon?"

"The demon is the easy part. Trust me. It's their taunts you have to resist."

"What do you mean?"

Derek looked to his young apprentice with a knowing smile.

"The biggest obstacle you will ever have to overcome, my friend, is yourself."

NOW

9

APRIL LAUGHED AND GAVE OSCAR A FRIENDLY PUSH.

"No, it's my turn," she insisted.

"Fine!" Oscar responded, smiling warmly at the woman of his dreams occupying the passenger seat in front of him.

"Right, would you rather..." April took a moment's thought. "I got it. Would you rather – watch your parents have sex, or have your parents watch you have sex?"

Oscar blurted out a stream of awkward laughter.

"And I can't pick neither?"

"No!" April grinned. "It's the game, you have to pick one."

"Okay, I guess... oh man. I'd rather watch them..."

Oscar pulled a face of disgust. April raised her eyebrows, playing at being perturbed.

"All right, here's one for you," Oscar took over. "Would you rather have hair that always stank of pee, or have breasts that could talk, but constantly argue with each other?"

"Oh man, that one's easy. Talking breasts all the way."

"Really?"

"Yeah! I always wondered what they'd say if they could talk."

Oscar chuckled. He looked into her eyes, and she looked

back. They held their eye contact in a moment of electricity, watching each other intently.

"I got one," Oscar spoke, coming up with an idea. "Would you rather date me, or date no one?"

April smiled so wide she practically glowed.

"I would rather date–"

The door to the driver's seat swung open and Julian threw himself into the car, scowling, not looking at anyone else. His bad mood was immediately apparent and an uncomfortable, tense silence took over the car.

With a regretful glance at Oscar, April turned around to face the front and put her seat belt on.

Cursing his luck, Oscar stared out the window. Julian turned the ignition and drove away, swinging them around the corner to the car park's exit. Oscar watched as the prison faded from view, and they were travelling between absent fields once more.

"What's up?" April quietly asked, looking to Julian.

"I don't want to talk about it," Julian snapped.

"But you're never in a bad mood after we've seen Derek. I don't get it."

"I said I don't want to talk about it!"

The next ten minutes passed without so much as grunt or a cough from anyone. Julian's eyes remained intently glaring at the road before him.

Oscar watched Julian, wondering what could have troubled him so much. Julian was always so excited to see Derek, it was hard to understand why he would be so irrefutably angry.

Maybe he'd had some bad news.

Maybe Derek had said something sad.

Or, maybe, this was just Julian being Julian. He was always so ill-tempered whenever he was around Oscar, to the point Oscar wasn't entirely sure if Julian had another range of emotions, or whether it was just Oscar that the problem was with.

Oscar had been meaning to enquire about Derek's incarceration on the ride home, but found himself wondering whether it was the right time. He needed to know why Derek was in there, what had happened, and about Derek's history.

But he dare not speak.

But then again, maybe, talking about Derek in a positive light would take Julian's mind off whatever he was ruminating about.

Oscar decided he was going to try to converse with Julian, figuring whatever he said or did seemed to annoy the guy anyway, so he didn't really have anything to lose.

"Hey, Julian," Oscar spoke, watching Julian's scowl turn to him in the rear-view mirror. "You know you said Derek is a war hero."

"He is," grunted Julian defensively.

"What war? What happened?"

Julian sighed with exasperation. He ran a hand over his face, frustrated at having to engage in what would likely turn into a long, embellished conversation. At that moment, he just wanted to remain in furious silence.

April gave him a wary glance.

"He has a right to know, Julian," she urged him.

"Fine," Julian mumbled.

Oscar waited a moment for Julian to gather his thoughts, watching and waiting with intrigue.

"He had a very close friend," Julian began. "This friend was a great exorcist, the greatest there has ever been. But he also had something evil within him. Derek trained him, then had to fight him."

"Evil? Like a demon?"

"Worse than a demon."

Oscar watched the fields go by the window, considering

this. To think – that weak, dishevelled man fought something as powerful as a prince of hell.

"But I don't get it. For such a great man, why is he in prison?" Oscar asked.

Julian took in a big, deep breath. His mouth moved as if he was trying to find the words, but was unable to force them out of his lips.

Oscar had never seen Julian stumped for words before.

"Derek took Julian to his first exorcism" – April took over, watching Julian breathe a sigh of relief that he didn't have to recollect this memory – "where they exorcised a young girl called Anna."

Oscar remembered April mentioning this girl before he witnessed Julian perform an exorcism for the first time. He remembered April telling him what happened.

"Oh," Oscar confirmed, understanding what Julian was finding so difficult to say.

"Derek was arrested for the girl's death," April continued. "The prosecution claimed that he let this girl, in his care, die. They said he didn't give her food or water, or rest. He was eventually charged with manslaughter by negligence, and sent to prison."

"And that's where he is now," Julian angrily interjected. "The man who saved this entire world from an apocalypse, stuck in jail to rot because the law doesn't take into account the reality of–"

Julian cut himself off. His fists were gripping the steering wheel and his leg was shaking. He willed himself to calm down.

Oscar nodded, and let them continue the rest of the journey in silence.

10

ANOTHER NIGHT, MORE LONG, RESTLESS HOURS OF CONSTANT shifting. Derek knew that the prison experience was intentionally uncomfortable, but surely giving them beds like this was against their human rights?

He could feel every square set of wires digging into his back, pressing against his bones. He tried sleeping on his side, but every morning he woke up in agony. It didn't help that he wasn't particularly in the best physical condition he'd ever been in.

Once, he'd even tried getting rid of the bumpy mattress altogether, but the indents of the solid metal frame were even worse. Some mornings he'd find himself waking up on the floor, having had a far better sleep because of it.

He tried listening carefully. It's what he'd always told those he taught – stop, listen to the elements, take them in. Allow them to relax your state of mind.

In the distance, he could hear an owl, roaming free, liberated to make noise and fly away at will.

The smell of stale urine accompanied the distant wails of someone in the midst of a mental breakdown.

No, paying attention to the elements did not help him here.

Eventually, he found himself drifting into a restless slumber, still unable to find peace in his sleep. His mind searched his unconscious for ways to torment his aching brain. Images of Anna taunted him; as if his incarceration wasn't enough, his guilt was even worse.

The thought of her still made him sick. A churning in his stomach twisted and turned every time he saw her face.

Like most nights, he watched as she died in the doctor's arms. Watched as she...

"Derek."

His eyes sprung open.

He bolted upright, sweating, looking back and forth.

No one was there. Just darkness.

It was his dream.

It must have been in his dream.

He couldn't let himself be paranoid, just because of what he knew about this world.

I've seen too much.

With knowledge like he had, he needed to be careful not to attribute ghosts to nothing.

But there was something. A scratching. Something from outside his cell.

Speaking.

Low, eerie speaking.

Derek twisted himself out of his bed and hoisted himself to his feet via the nearby sink. Grabbing his walking stick, he hobbled to the edge of his cell and peered into the corridor.

He occupied cell twenty-five of A Wing. Opposite him, and to his left and right, were at least forty cells. The wing carried on above him into three more floors, home to a similar number of prisoners. It was a category B prison, meaning most of the inmates were in for violent offences, and he often had to ensure he remained withdrawn from conflict and bullying that occurred. Each cell had a narrow single bed, a television with a small screen, a metal sink, and a metal toilet with no seat. It was the minimum they were allowed.

The bars to the cells were dark blue, the floor a dark brown, and the walls a light cream colour. The walls of the wing and the cells caused every movement to echo, meaning Derek could clearly hear any scuffle occurring along the corridor, however small or insignificant. The scuttle of a rat could sound like the feet of a giant, if he let it.

Peering as far as he could through the bars, Derek saw a few figures beside the entrance to a cell a few down from his, at what was known as the segregation cells. These were the cells where prisoners were sent to be separated and watched, either for their protection or someone else's.

"Get on your feet, old man," came a gruff voice. Derek recognised it as that of the prison governor, Jackson Kullins.

On his feet before the governor was one of Derek's very few acquaintances, Sully. Sully and Derek often shared silent lunches, becoming friendly on the basis that they were the two eldest on the wing. Sully was still Derek's senior by a long way, Derek estimating Sully to be in his late seventies. He had never asked, nor had he ever asked what Sully was in for, a gesture that was unspoken and mutual.

"I said get on your feet," Kullins barked in a snarling whisper.

Sully struggled to his feet, his weak bones and soft hands unable to support his weight. As soon as his wobbling knees had taken him to his feet, Kullins kicked them out again, sending Sully slamming onto his back.

Kullins spat at Sully.

"That's what you are," Kullins told the poor old man. He watched as two prison officers dragged him back into his cell, grunting another obscenity that Derek couldn't make out.

Kullins's face suddenly shot in Derek's direction, and Derek retracted back into his cell with a gasp. He struggled to his bed as quick as his aching legs could take him, hearing the governor's footsteps growing nearer.

He returned to his bed, laying on his side and facing the wall as he heard the footsteps pause beside his cell. They stopped, hovered for a moment, then left. Derek kept his eyes closed until he heard the door to the wing shut.

"Derek."

His head spun around once more.

Something whispered his name again.

"Derek."

He searched his cell with his weary eyes, looking in every dark corner, every which way he could.

"You are in danger, you need to leave."

He spun to his feet, looking around.

Nothing.

"Who's there?" he whispered.

He listened intently.

Waited for a response in the eerie silence.

Nothing.

Probably the hallucination of an ageing mind.

Or, something trying to warn him. Maybe someone he used to know, giving him an omen, suggesting that he find a way to escape.

Either way, it could wait until morning.

He wasn't going anywhere.

He lay down and closed his eyes, hoping that Sully was okay.

11

ANOTHER COFFEE, ANOTHER CAFÉ, ANOTHER AWKWARD conversation.

Oscar couldn't understand what was causing him so much stress.

It's just a girl, right?

Men have been admitting their affections for girls since the dawn of time.

Well, technically, man didn't evolve at the dawn of time, dinosaurs did. And, actually, when man originally evolved into cavemen, they didn't admit their affection, they just clobbered the girl they fancied over the head and dragged them into a cave.

It was a much simpler time.

Not that Oscar intended to clobber April over the head and drag her into a cave. In fact, having thought about it, the whole concept was actually quite wrong.

What the hell is wrong with me? I'm sitting here opposite the woman I fancy in silence as I daydream about bloody cavemen...

"So," Oscar began, before abruptly realising he hadn't thought through how he was going to complete that sentence.

"So," April repeated in anticipation, taking a sip of hot chocolate, then wiping a bit of cream off her nose.

Ooh, what I'd give to be that bit of cream.

Hang on.

What? I'd like to be wiped off her nose?

Oscar hung his head in a mixture of confused shame and anxious apprehension.

"So, how long have we known each other?" he blurted out, louder and quicker than he had intended.

"Didn't you ask me this the other day?"

"Yeah, yeah, I did…" Oscar nodded, unsure how to respond. "But, er… I didn't get a chance to finish it."

He took a big deep breath, let it out, then took a large sip of his coffee. He held the coffee by his mouth and took a longer sip than he wanted, anything to avoid having to confront the chaotic words that were pushing against the inside of his lips.

"What's up, Oscar?" April asked. "You look nervous."

"Nervous? Look nervous? I'm not nervous. Who's nervous? Are you nervous?"

"Oscar, you're being a little weird."

He went to speak, nodded, held his breath, and took another large, drawn-out sip of coffee.

"You're really cool, aren't you? I mean, you're not going to say you're cool, but you are. Cool, I mean."

"Okay. So we've established I'm cool…"

"Yeah, yeah, we have. I'm glad we've established that."

He took another elongated sip of coffee, to find that he was out of coffee, and panicked.

"I wanted to talk about us. As in, you and me."

"Okay," April urged him, smiling, wanting him to continue.

"Well." Oscar took another big, deep breath. Went to drink his coffee again, forgetting that the cup was empty, and ended up poising the cup by his mouth to disguise the fact that the coffee was gone.

"Isn't your cup empty?"

Oscar froze, dropped his coffee cup to the table, and looked in it.

"Oh, yeah. That explains why no coffee was coming out."

"So, you were saying?" April prompted him, raising her eyebrows expectantly, willing him to finish.

"Well. I think you're cool, as you know."

"Yes, we have confirmed this."

"Good, I – I'm glad. Now, I just, ghosts and stuff, they are scary, but what I'm feeling in my gut, is, also, erm, scary. I mean, not in the same way, just..."

He paused.

Stared at his empty coffee cup.

Looked at April, her wide, beautiful eyes gazing back at him, her long, flowing hair brushing down her shoulders like the wind down a mountain. Her skin was perfect, her fashion sense was perfect, her personality was perfect, she...

She's too perfect for me.

He shook his head.

He was kidding himself.

A woman like this would never go for a guy like him.

"Never mind," he muttered, staring into the black abyss of his mug.

"Never mind?" April asked, disappointment in her voice.

"Yeah... Never mind..."

Oscar only saw April's crestfallen face out the corner of his eye. She finished her drink and stood.

"I guess I'd better get going then," she told him, evidently dejected. She was out of her seat and through the door before he could muster any form of objection.

Oscar, you complete and utter arse.

He hung his head and mentally scolded himself.

Was he ever going to get a grip?

1 2

THE CEILING ABOVE JULIAN'S BED HAD BECOME A FAMILIAR SIGHT. He lay sleepily and with vague thoughts, in the midst of another sleepless night, enduring hours and hours of staring until its dark cream colour morphed into an indefinite blur. He traced the familiar indents with his eyes, following the same cracks, to the same cobwebs hanging loosely in the corner, absent of an owner. He was fairly sure that, should he ever be required, he would be able to draw an accurate picture of its various bumps and indentations, and the various shades cast upon it by the moon peering through a narrow crack in the curtains.

He would kill to fall asleep, yet, at the same time, he dreaded it.

Staying awake meant his mind dwelled on the eyes of that same young girl being drained of life; but falling asleep meant her pale face plagued his nightmares.

It was affecting him, and even worse, it was affecting his work.

Derek had taught him to be a thorough professional. To be presentable, courteous, and do the best job you can. Yet, more recently, he had found himself growing snappy and irritable. He was aware he already had some instinctive impatience, and so dreaded to consider how he must inevitably be coming across.

He closed his eyes. Willed the bad thoughts away.

Why now?

Why was it, after four years, the memories of Anna were only now surfacing so severely?

That night had attacked his memory numerous times since, but it had been a black cloud he could control. It gave him resilience, whilst reminding him what was at stake. Before every exorcism, every cleansing, every supernatural ritual, he would remember her. She would remind him of what he could lose – and that knowledge had made him a thorough, scrupulous, professional paranormal investigator.

He had never let a situation get to the point that Anna's exorcism did.

He opened his eyes.

Glanced at the clock.

3.05 a.m.

Was it really that late?

Have I really been lying here, dozing in and out of consciousness, constantly thinking, for four hours?

He swivelled himself around and leant on the edge of the bed.

There were sleeping tablets in the drawer of the kitchen.

They were the last resort. It was never good to rely on pills to get you to sleep, and Julian hated having to do it. But it was the only way.

I need sleep... Desperately...

He stood, wiping sweat from his brow. The bedroom was sticky hot, to the point that the duvet was sticking to his bare torso.

59

He opened the bedroom door and stepped into the living room of his flat.

A wave of frozen air hit him.

His high temperature instantly plummeted. His skin grew goose pimples, his shoulders shuddered, and his hands shivered, overwhelmed by a sudden and unexpected change from extreme humidity to unbearable cold.

He made his way across the living room and to the kitchen, shivering, rubbing his arms, trying to generate heat.

That's when he realised.

If he was investigating somewhere...

If he was looking for signs of an entity in a home...

Then a sudden drop in temperature would be a major factor he'd be looking to consider.

No.

Don't be ridiculous.

Yes, sudden changes in temperature, rooms that have an unexpected cold compared to the rest of the location – that is a sign of an entity dwelling within.

But the sign was one of many. It would take numerous indications to confirm anything. Julian prided himself on being obsessively scientific when it came to confirming whether a location was home to a dangerous presence. A change in temperature was a sure sign, yes, but would not be enough as an isolated symptom.

He couldn't let his mind run away from him just because of what he knew and what he'd seen.

He opened the cupboard beneath the sink and sifted through a bunch of medicine boxes. He found a pack of sleeping aids, popped two, and placed them in his mouth.

He took a small glass out of the cupboard, filled it with water, looked up, and–

He dropped the glass, smashing it on the floor beside his bare feet.

He looked away, shook his head, looked back.

It was nothing.

Nothing was there.

But I swear I saw...

In the reflection of the kitchen window, his own face looked back at him.

But he had seen...

Anna...

Her face...

The still, dead eyes of her corpse...

No. Stop it.

It was a tired mind playing tired tricks. All that stared back at him in that reflection was his own pair of eyes and horrified face. He had seen nothing. It was a passing trick of his feeble state of mind; that was all.

And now there was broken glass on his feet.

"Shit," he muttered angrily.

He found a dustpan and brush from the drawer, swept the glass, and put it in the bin. He bypassed the glass and took a mouthful of water straight from the tap, then swallowed the pills.

Shaking his head to himself, he returned to the bedroom, having one last glance over his shoulder at the window.

Nothing was there.

It was just a painful memory.

Tricks of the mind.

There was nothing strong enough to indicate anything untoward occurring.

Be scientific.

He returned to the sweltering heat of his bedroom, climbed into bed and closed his eyes, waiting for the tablets to take effect.

THEN

13

Julian gazed around Derek's study in astonishment. The vast collection of books demonstrated physically Derek's immense resources and incredible knowledge. Everything you could ever want to know about the paranormal was in a large shelving unit against a wall in his study.

"This" – Derek began, opening a hefty, worn-out, leather-bound book, forcing a hundred particles of dust to float into the air – "is called *The Rites of Exorcism*. This has everything you need to know."

Julian peered over Derek's shoulder.

"Is this what you will be using on that girl?" Julian asked. "Anna, I think her name was?"

"Yes, these are the prayers I will recite. They are the prayers I have recited for years. Before you were even born, I imagine."

Julian raised his eyebrows in bewilderment. He never ceased to be amazed.

"Care to take a look?"

Derek smiled at Julian, standing back so he could see.

Julian placed his hand on the page. It had a brown tint, and the paper was thin from age. The act of an exorcism was an ancient art, he knew that – but he had never contemplated how ancient the book would have been.

He slowly traced his forefinger over the first line of a prayer written in an old font, immaculately preserved.

IN THE NAME of Jesus Christ, our God and Lord, strengthened by the intercession of the Immaculate Virgin Mary, Mother of God, of Blessed Michael the Archangel, so the wicked perish at the presence of God.

"Wow," Julian unknowingly whispered.

"Why 'wow'?" Derek asked, prompting Julian to abruptly realise he had spoken.

"It's just, it's so… preachy. Religious. I've never really gone in for this kind of stuff."

"Neither have I. And despite having seen what I have seen, I question those who do."

"You mean, you fight in God's name, but judge those who believe in God? How does that make sense?"

A warm grin spread across Derek from cheek to cheek, pleased that Julian was asking the right questions.

"You still need to approach this with a scientific mind – you believe something once you can't prove otherwise. I have seen angels, demons, even the devil himself. I have seen enough to know for certain. But people who follow this stuff blindly without having seen a shred of true, undeniable evidence?" Derek shrugged his shoulders. "Ninety-nine percent of the potential possessions I visit are mental health issues interpreted by a highly religious family. So rarely is it ever the real thing. I believe people could use a tad more scrutiny with their thinking."

Julian nodded. It was a lot to take in, though it made a lot of sense. It must be frustrating to visit continual claims of hauntings that turn out to be nothing.

Or so he'd find out when he took on the role of exorcist himself someday.

"Let me show you another chapter," Derek decided. He bent over the book and began sifting through pages.

As he did that, Julian wandered over to the impressive book collection, looking across the titles. There was everything from mediumship, telling the difference between psychosis and genuine possession, seances, exorcism through the ages – any topic that could be covered was there.

Then something caught his eye.

A small book hidden behind two larger books. He reached between them and pulled it out, surveying the spine with his curious eyes.

The author was Derek Lansdale.

How peculiar, Derek never mentioned writing a book...

He pulled it out and looked at the cover, reading the title quietly to himself.

My Journal of The Edward King War.

"Hey, Derek?" Julian spoke, turning toward his mentor.

"Yes?" Derek replied, lifting his eyes up.

"What's this? What's the Edward King war?" Julian asked, lifting the book.

Derek's face instantly dropped. It turned cold, melancholy, petrified even. A wash of terror swept over his face.

"Where did you find that?" Derek gasped.

"It was wedged between two bigger books. I just thought–"

Julian had no time to finish the sentence. Derek snatched the book out of his hands and cradled it in his arms, hugging it tightly so there was no way Julian could get to it.

"Sorry, Derek, I didn't mean..."

"It's fine," Derek lied. "Just – look at the book I told you to look at."

Derek scurried out of the room and pounded up the stairs.

Julian was left standing there, wondering what he had just witnessed.

NOW

1 4

A BRUSH AGAINST DEREK'S FACE MADE HIM INSTINCTIVELY WAVE his hand to waft it away.

He turned onto his other side, groaning, irritated at being awakened. He allowed his mind to sink further into his unconscious, returning to the emptiness of a heavy slumber

It came again. Something brushing. Sweeping past his cheek.

It was the same, but different.

Before, it had felt like a faint touch, barely pricking his skin. Like a feather softly caressing him.

The second time, he could feel something. Something stronger, something definite, pressing with a gentle but sinister force. Something fleetingly placed against his cheek with four soft indents.

Something that felt like…

His eyes flickered. His mind stirred.

Something that felt like fingers.

"Go away," he grunted, his sleepy state not fully acknowledging the occurrence. Whoever was trying to wake him could return in the morning.

He allowed his heavy eyelids to remain shut, pressing together with the desperate ease of a tired mind.

Hang on.

His eyes shot open.

He was in a locked cell.

Someone had touched his cheek.

He was in a locked cell, and someone had touched his cheek.

He sat up, looking around.

The full moon was high in the sky, casting little light through the narrow window at the top of his cell. He cast his eyes around the narrow room, peering across the small, confined space.

He was alone.

Alone in his cell, as he had been when he'd settled down to sleep.

Had he really felt that?

Had it just been part of his sleep? A trick of the mind?

He shook his head.

No.

I've seen enough to know when something is just a trick of the mind.

Too much was happening. And it was all too convenient that it was happening to him.

"Who's there?" he asked. It had been a while since he had tried to contact something not of this world. Years, even. His voice sounded a lot older and weaker than it had the last time he'd attempted to open communication with the dead or the demonic.

But he was not afraid.

He had been to hell.

Twice.

He'd seen enough to know how to battle these things.

Except, that was before. That was when he was full of

energy, youthful exuberance, and fighting at the side of a friend who had enough powers to return him back to earth.

That was nothing like now.

He was an incarcerated inmate who required a walking stick just to be able to plod the short but long journey from his cell to the medical wing.

He wasn't in the best condition of his life, and he knew it.

A soft brush pressed against the back of his top; an easy breeze fixed against his clothes.

He didn't move.

He waited. Listened.

Remained desperately immobile.

It came again, pushing his back, turning from a slight press of air to something definite, pushing against him.

It pushed hard, growing more forceful until he could feel the indentations of each specific finger pressing against his shoulder blade.

He leapt to his feet and spun around, ready to confront whatever was there.

But nothing was there.

Nothing.

Something moved in the corner of his eye. Something outside the cell. Something dark and silhouetted.

"I repeat, who is there?" he asked the silence, his voice echoing with adamant gumption.

Nothing happened.

"Of all the people you can haunt, trust me, I am the last man you want to mess with," he declared with the confidence of someone who could back his statement up.

Something flickered once again out the corner of his eye.

A figure moved past his cell, so fast that if he had blinked, he would have missed it. He wasn't looking directly at it, so couldn't be sure of what he had seen, but he could vaguely recall a large, looming, shadowy figure, with long fingers and a thin, contorted head.

He strode the few paces it took to get to the bars of his cell, ignoring the pain in his limp as he dragged his heavy leg.

"Who's there?" he whispered, careful not to wake the other prisoners – he was cautious as to what they would do to him in the morning if he interrupted their rest.

He strained to look across the walls of the wing. The place was in complete darkness, and his view was restricted by the wall of his cell.

It can't hurt me.

He repeated it to himself again and again.

It can't hurt me. It can't hurt me.

He wondered whether he was reassuring himself of the truth, or trying to convince himself of a lie.

As if providing him with his answer, he was launched across the cell, through the air, hitting the far wall with a painful thud. His back cracked against the solid stone and he fell into a helpless slump on the floor.

His bad leg throbbed. Even though it was his back that had made the worst contact with the wall, it was his leg that pulsated with agonising intensity.

A delayed ache in his back shortly joined it.

It felt like he had more bones than he had before, each of them hurting, excruciating from the impact.

It can hurt me.

He remained where he was, frightened that if he were to try and get to his feet he would either fail, or the entity would force him onto his back once more.

So he stayed in a messy ball on the floor, staring at the end of the cell. Watching. Waiting.

Waiting for something, or someone, to appear, and to confront him.

Whatever it was.

Whatever it could be.

The ghost of a murdered ex-prisoner?

The dead child of a prison birth?

Or a demon seeking vengeance against Derek. Something that wanted revenge for being exorcised, and knew that Derek was trapped with nowhere to go.

There would be plenty of them.

But nothing came.

His mind was full of loose speculations that did not materialise as he stared at the dark, empty void of A Wing.

He remained fixed in his position, glaring at the doors to the cell, waiting for something to reveal itself. To show him what he was up against. To fill him with dread.

He awoke in the morning when the prison officer came to open his cell.

15

Oscar was starting to get the hang of this.

It was another house savaged by another spirit that refused to move on.

Which makes sense, really. I mean, if you were dead, would you want to move on? Or would you do everything you could to stay on this earth?

Denial is the most common human trait, yet the most counterproductive.

And here he was, at another routine cleansing, in a previously tranquil family home, with an angry, uneasy spirit. April had placed burning sage in the middle of the living room, Julian had cast a circle of salt around the outside of the house, and Oscar was stood, prepared for what he counted as his twelfth cleansing, going over his words in his mind.

The room was dark and empty. Furniture had been moved elsewhere so that it couldn't shake and cause damage. Photo frames had been removed, as faces provided access to the evil spirits they fought. And any loose items that could be picked up or thrown were in a few boxes in the hallway. The residents of the house waited patiently in the dining room.

Oscar, April, and Julian were alone – well, alone in the sense that they were the only people who were alive in the room.

April closed her eyes and bowed her head, sitting cross-legged on the floor.

This was the part that put lumps in Oscar's belly. He knew April was an expert conduit and had done this many, many times – but he still worried that she wouldn't return. That when she allowed her body to be used as a vessel, the entity that entered her would refuse to let her body go. He had to remind himself that she was in control. Just so long as he did his prayers and recited the incantations correctly, she would remain the one in control.

He hadn't failed her yet, and he did not intend to.

Julian watched April, waiting as she fell into a deep trance.

"We call on the spirit within this house." Julian spoke calmly and assertively, standing opposite April, the burning sage between them. "I ask you to use this woman as your vessel, to allow us to speak to you."

He waited.

It rarely happened the first time.

Spirits were normally hesitant to engage in direct conversation with the residents of the house they were reluctant to leave, but Oscar had seen this numerous times – they always surfaced eventually.

"I repeat, the spirit within this house, use April as a vessel to speak to us."

Oscar looked around himself.

Julian paused.

Nothing.

"I repeat, spirit in this house–"

A gust of wind burst past Oscar, past Julian, and against April's chest. She seized a few times, shook, then allowed her head to lift, her eyes still closed.

"Spirit, my name is Julian. Please tell me yours."

They waited a few moments in eerie silence, staring at April, awaiting the spirit's response.

"My name" – she spoke in a voice distinctly not hers; it was that of an old, grumpy man, the kind of cynical old man who was impatient and hated everything – "my name is none of your business."

"Spirit, I have given you mine. It is only fair you give me yours."

"Leave this house," came the blunt response.

"I'm afraid I cannot do that."

Oscar readied himself.

It was nearly his part.

As soon as they had the spirit in a vulnerable state, as soon as it realised it was no longer alive, that it needed to move on, that's when he would say the prayers. The prayers that would cleanse April of the host, and the house of its spirit.

April could keep the entity within her long enough for Oscar to expel it.

"Spirit, I have some bad news for you."

An angry groan escaped April.

"You are dead," Julian spoke.

April's lips remained sealed.

"I repeat, spirit, you are dead. Surely you must realise this."

"You lie."

"I do not lie, I promise you. You are dead, and you need to move on."

"This is my home!"

"Not anymore. In life, yes, but in death… You no longer belong in this world, spirit."

"No!"

Julian gave a nod to Oscar.

"It is time for you to leave."

"No! I will never leave!"

Julian lifted his cross toward April.

"No! No! Get it away!"

Oscar stood forward.

"I know my transgressions, and my sin is ever before me," Oscar began, full of confidence. This was his part and he loved it. Loved being able to expel something from someone's body. He knew a demon would be way too powerful for him – that's what a trained exorcist like Julian was for – but a dead person refusing to leave this world; that was something he could deal with. "Against you, you alone, I have sinned. Indeed, I was born guilty, but I hide my face from your sins, and blot out all my iniquities."

"No! No! What are you doing?" cried the old man.

Julian smiled. It was working.

"Create in me a clean heart, oh God, and put a new and right spirit within this woman."

"No! Stop it!"

"In the name, power and authority of Jesus Christ, Lord and Saviour God, Holy Ghost, do the work I need right now, as I make these proclamations."

"Stop!"

"I renounce and reject all sins, and I–"

He stuttered.

"And I–"

Shit.

The words escaped Oscar. Fell out of his mind like water through fingers.

"And I – I..."

The old man cackled.

"You foolish boy..."

Julian shot Oscar a look of lividity, pure anger surging from his eyes.

"And I... shit..."

"Oscar, say the prayer."

79

"I... I've forgotten it..."

"Say the damn prayer!"

"I can't! I forgot!"

"I will never leave!" declared the old man.

"He's going to take April, say the prayer!"

"I can't!"

"Say the fucking prayer, Oscar!"

"..."

Julian shoved Oscar out of the way and stood over April's body, pressing the cross against her head.

"I renounce and reject any sinful items kept here," Julian took over.

The old man writhed in pain.

"I renounce and reject any sinful things broadcast within this house, and within this body," Julian continued.

"No!"

"I renounce and reject sinful evil within this host!"

April stiffened like a plank for a few moments, then flopped onto the floor.

Julian dove to her side, shaking her, willing her eyes to open. Eventually, they did.

Oscar rushed to their side.

"Is she okay?"

"Fuck off, Oscar!" Julian shouted, a venomous glare of detest aimed in his direction.

Oscar backed away.

"April, are you okay?" Julian shook her once more.

Her eyes feebly blinked, and Julian helped her sit up, leaning her against the sofa. She rubbed her face, coming around, and finally readjusted to the room.

Julian stood and faced Oscar.

Oscar was stuck to the spot, looking wide-eyed and terrified from April to Julian, to April, to Julian.

"April, I'm so sorry," Oscar genuinely lamented.

"Don't you dare, you complete, bloody imbecile," Julian snapped.

"Julian, don't," April pleaded. "It's fine."

"No, it's not!" Julian shouted, not removing his glare from a desperately anxious Oscar. "Do you know what you could have done?"

"I didn't mean to–"

"Of course you didn't, but that's the worst part, isn't it? You didn't mean to, you just happen to be a fucking moron."

"Julian!" April cried out, taken aback at the words pouring out of Julian's mouth.

"You are not worth my time, and you will never amount to shit, you complete and utter fucking liability!" Julian was now screaming.

"I'm sorry!" Oscar cried, covering his face.

"Julian, that's enough!" April demanded.

No one moved. They remained in angry, stone-cold silence.

"I'm going to go tell the woman who lives here we've been successful," Julian decided, finally breaking the absence of noise and leaving the room. "I daren't give you another job you might fuck up."

Oscar and April shared a look. A look in which Oscar could tell he had let her down.

"I'll wait in the car," he told her and left, hanging his head in shame, wondering if there would ever be anything he could do that he would not screw up.

16

JULIAN CHARGED OUT OF THE HOUSE, CLENCHED FISTS, MAKING A beeline to the car.

Oscar shamefully followed. April watched him as he dragged his feet out of the house, head hung, eyes low, like a puppy who's lost their owner. She knew Oscar well enough to know that this wasn't him making a scene; if anything, this was him doing his best not to. He didn't want anyone to know how much he had let himself down.

It had been an unpleasant experience, but he did not deserve Julian's ill-tempered rant.

He was young. He was new. Yes, he'd had a fair bit of field experience, but he was still learning at a faster rate than either she or Julian had.

It wasn't fair.

"Oscar, just wait here," she told him, pausing him outside the front door.

He faked a smile, unable to look her in the eyes.

She took hold of his hand, knowing how much her touch meant to him, and he met her eyes.

"I'm fine, Oscar. Honestly," she reassured him. "Just – hang on."

He hesitantly nodded, his wounded look still fixed to his face. He was trying to conceal it, trying to put a brave mask on – but she knew him well enough by now.

Having persuaded Oscar to remain put, she stormed down the driveway toward the car, where Julian was opening the car door. April intercepted it and slammed it shut, glaring at his eyes, those eyes that had previously been so caring. Something had changed in him over the last few days, and she did not know what it was, but it did not excuse him talking to Oscar like that. She had to stand up to him.

Even if it was the first time in her life she'd ever had to stand up to such a close, faithful friend.

"What the hell is wrong with you?" she barked.

"What do you mean?" he demanded, bending down to meet her glare with his, a venom in his voice she had never heard before.

"He's just a kid!"

"Yes, he is just a kid. It's time he grew up. He could have done some serious damage to you in there."

"But he didn't!"

"But he could have!"

She shook her head and folded her arms, pursing her lips, doing her best to contain her fury.

"Don't you dare try and pretend that was for my benefit. Not a single bit of that was for my protection. It was for your own ego, against someone who so blatantly looks up to you. You love him feeding out of your hand, don't you?"

"Oh, sorry, am I going to offend your useless little boyfriend?"

He barged her out the way with his shoulder, opened the car door, and threw himself into the driver's seat. As he started the engine, he went to close the door, to find April stood in the way once more, her arms still folded and her scowl intensifying.

"Move out of the way, April."

"No." She shook her head.

He huffed. She knew he would not shove her completely out of the way. There would be no way he could apologise for pushing her.

"Do you know what? You deserve him!" he exclaimed. "Both of you are little kids, who have no idea what it's like to live in this real world. I cannot stop dreaming about Anna. Do you have any idea what that is like? What it's like to see that every night? No, because you've never had to deal with the real repercussions of what these things can do to people!"

"Shut up, Julian. I've been channelling enough evil things to know the reality of this world."

"Yeah? Try having a kid die on you."

Tense silence ensued.

Was that what this was about?

Because she hadn't had a kid like Anna die on her?

And it was her fault she hadn't had that experience? That meant she knew nothing?

No.

It couldn't be.

She knew Julian. She knew this wasn't about her, or Oscar – it was about him. Something was going on.

Normally, she could read him so well. But now...

He was panting. His eyes were breaking. He would consider himself too manly to cry openly in front of her, she knew that, but she could see it in his eyes. That little boy inside breaking, shattering to pieces and fading away like smoke.

"This isn't you," April told him, lowering her voice, trying to be soothing and calm, rather than heated and angry. "You're direct, that's what you're like; that's fine. But you've never been this bad."

He shook his head. Slammed his hands on the steering wheel. His face was breaking, and he was desperate to leave the situation, April could see that. But she wasn't letting him go anywhere.

"Get out of the way, April," he instructed, putting his hand on the door handle.

"No."

He sighed.

"Do you know what Derek once told me?"

"What?"

"The biggest obstacle you ever have to overcome is yourself."

And with that, he shoved her, closed the door, and drove away.

Within seconds, Oscar was at her side.

"How are we going to get home now?" he innocently mused.

Julian had taken her off the street when she was a teenager. Taught her everything she knew. She couldn't bear to have him upset or mad at her.

She turned and pushed herself into Oscar's arms, covering her face, feeling his warm embrace wrap around her.

THEN

17

A CALM BREEZE FLUTTERED THROUGH THE OPEN WINDOW, filling the room with a summer glow. The sound of birds singing to each other, children laughing as they cycled past, a postman whistling a jaunty tune – it all sauntered so eagerly through Julian's mind.

But Julian's mind was nothing like the scene outside.

Inside his head it was a tsunami. Angry faces bickering, turning to green and red, phasing away into horned beasts and wicked grins. Storms plunged from grey clouds, peeking from the corners of his mind into his melancholy solace.

His hand absently fiddled with a two-pence coin, turning it around between his thumb and his forefinger, spinning it, then tapping it against the desk.

His tired eyes lingered outside the window, scalding the happy scenes, willing the mothers to take their kids away and hide them from the dark recesses of this world.

Demons existed.

Ghosts existed.

The devil existed.

Everything he had thought untrue. Everything he had

argued against. Everything those irrational religious minds had sworn to him. Everything he had deplored through various statuses on social media about the ridiculous wars caused by religion.

It was real. And he felt foolish.

How they would laugh at him now!

How they would mock him and ridicule him, sneer at him for his upturned nose, shake their heads at his ignorant, uneducated mind.

And to them, he would sneer right back.

Because they praise their God. They worship him.

They have no idea what God can do.

He could remove a demon from a child. Once the exorcist had tested their faith, and proven their devotion, and God willingly lent his hand in removing the entity, then that child would be saved.

And what happened should God not be willing? Should God not approve the test of dedication?

Anna.

That's what happened.

He slammed the coin down on the table and shifted position, as if he was about to get up and do something. Make a stand. Volunteer a contribution to society. Do something that would make a difference; that would change what happened.

Yet he remained static. The bones of his rear end shifting uncomfortably against the solid wooden seat of his kitchen. Mentally deploring the world parading by his window.

Because there was nothing he could do.

He could stand and try, but so what?

She was dead.

Dead.

Dead, dead, dead.

A young girl robbed of the right to grow old. A young girl's future taken away, her innocence ravaged, her sparkling smile replaced with a pale, vacant, stone-cold face.

Her eyes.

Those bloody eyes.

Those bloody, shitty, fucking eyes.

They stared at him.

And he did nothing but stare back.

Stare into their nothingness. Because there was nothing he could do.

He could make a stand against the rest of the demons. Against anything else that tried to take a child's life. Anything else that ever tried to consume one of God's children.

God.

He grunted a sarcastic laugh.

He would plead for His strength. He would beg for His mercy. He would pray to Him, beg for Him to take victims from their demons.

But Julian would never respect Him.

Because He did nothing.

Because God did not deem Derek's words faithful enough. Because Derek, a man who had literally fought and killed in His name for decades, did not pass the test.

Fuck him.

There was nothing more to think. Nothing more to say.

Anna was dead.

And with it, the soul of his mentor left too.

NOW

18

THE DEAD OF NIGHT ENCAPSULATED THE PRISON IN A CLOAK OF darkness. The half-moon barely shone through the window of Derek's cell, meaning he had a large shadow to work in.

Good. Darkness works better.

He sat on the floor, keeping himself calm, readying himself for what was to come. He was strong enough at contacting the paranormal elements that it wouldn't take him much, but it would take its toll on his weary body. His injuries, added to his aching bones and stiffened muscles, made him less responsive. But he was still determined to do this.

He lit a small tealight candle he'd acquired through paying another prisoner to smuggle it in for him. It wasn't the burning sage, the circle of salt, or the large candles he would normally require for a cleansing, but it would be enough for someone of his abilities.

At least, he hoped it would be.

He bowed his head and opened his lips into a barely audible whisper. If he was to do this, he needed to remain undisturbed, as an interruption would not only get him in trouble, but it would break his focus and ultimately the process.

"Holy Spirit," he began, "Thou make me see everything, and show me which way to reach my ideal. Thou who give me the divine gift to forgive and forget the wrong that is done to me and who is in all instances of my life with me. I pray, Holy Spirit, please show me the unclean spirits that haunt this cell."

He waited.

Nothing.

He bowed his head and closed his eyes, ensuring he remained calm, focussed, and completely at peace.

"Holy Spirit," he continued in his hushed voice, "with thy mercy, allow me to see what it is that dwells within this prison."

He opened his eyes.

This often took a while, he told himself. Just need to be patient.

Just need to remain calm.

"Holy Spirit, I–"

A swift brush of air against his face interrupted him. Slowly, he raised his head, opening his eyes.

Even after all this time, he still looked upon responsive spirits in disbelief that they answered his call.

"Hello, my name is Derek," he introduced himself. "What's yours?"

"Elizabeth," answered an apparition forming before him from a mixture of mist and smoke. It was a young woman, dressed in attire from before the prison was built. Her brown hair hung over her shoulders. She had an innocent smile and a long, dark-orange gown. Derek estimated the fifteenth century, based on the images of history he had studied.

"Elizabeth, thank you for responding to me," Derek spoke.

Elizabeth did not say a word. She hovered in the cell before him, a translucent figure hanging with the freedom of death.

"Elizabeth, why are you here?" Derek asked. "I don't imagine you were in this prison at any point, were you?"

"No."

"I would predict that you died before this prison was built, am I correct?

"Yes."

"Were you murdered?"

"Yes."

"Elizabeth, I appreciate your answers, but can you tell me anything else? Anything about this prison? About why you haunt it?"

The apparition hung her head. Derek thought he saw a gentle sob, but couldn't be sure. After an extended period of thinking time, she raised her head again. Derek willed himself to be patient, to see what she had to say.

"You are in danger," she told him bluntly.

"Me?"

"Yes."

"What about the other prisoners here? Are they in danger too?"

She hung her head once more.

"Are they in danger from you, Elizabeth?" he asked.

She didn't respond. She simply continued to hang her head in subdued silence.

"Are you going to hurt them?"

After a moment's hesitation, she shook her head, and lifted it once more to look Derek in the eyes.

"It is Jackson Kullins, the prison governor, that you need to fear."

"The governor? Why?"

She forced a solemn smile as she began to fade.

"No, please, Elizabeth, don't go. I need to ask you–"

But it was too late.

The spirit had faded into the darkness.

The tealight flickered before him, burning out and turning

into a string of smoke fading into the air and mixing with the moisture of his cell.

Derek didn't move.

He stared into the darkness where she had manifested herself, watching the shadows rest still in the cell before him.

19

Yet another sleepless night sent Julian's mind into a swirl of chaotic memories that clashed and spun until it was a storm he could no longer make sense of.

Julian lay on his back, staring at the ceiling, feeling the hours go by. He willed himself to close his eyes, to get some rest, to fall asleep, but they wouldn't shut. No matter how much he urged himself to sleep, his mind would not rest.

The covers lay in a crumpled mess around his knees, his bare torso sweating in the heat of the room. It was just this one room, just the bedroom that was this hot. The rest of the flat was so cold he could see his breath in the air. No matter what he did with the heating, no matter how he adjusted the radiators, nothing would fix the drastic change in temperature.

He tried closing his eyes. They were so heavy, so ready for sleep, but his mind wasn't. His thoughts bounced from manic recollections to parasitic images – that first exorcism projected onto the cinema screen of his mind, repeating itself as if the film reel was broken.

"Julian."

He lifted his head. Looked around the room.

The vague light from the moon seeped through a crack in the curtains, allowing him enough light to see that the room was empty. The corners were coated in still shadows, fixed and unfazed.

"Julian."

It came again.

A whisper so faint he wasn't entirely sure if he had heard it.

Tired minds cause tired hallucinations.

His thoughts were so incessant. Every night, the same damn images. The same twist in his gut, the same retching feeling crawling up the inside of his throat, the same sound of silence that pounded his eardrums with incessant ferocity. His concentration dwelled so exclusively on this one girl, that he was bound to start conjuring up sounds and images in his unconscious.

Still, he was curious.

The voice was so hushed he couldn't be sure who it belonged to. It was a vague whisper, barely audible, so much so it could easily have been the wind or a brush of his leg against the duvet.

He sat up, turning his legs out of bed and placing his bare feet on the warm carpet.

He took the glass of water from beside him, taking a big sip, drinking gulp, after gulp, after gulp.

The time read 3.08 a.m.

He placed the empty glass on his bedside table and paused. Resting. Listening. Waiting to hear something conclusive, something definite, something he could incontrovertibly attribute to something not of this world.

Nothing.

Just the silence of an empty flat.

Now I need the bloody toilet.

He stood, treading lightly out of his room, and taking the few slow steps across the living room to the bathroom.

He paused as he did, watching, waiting. The room was as he'd left it. A book placed on the sofa in a way that would preserve his page. His hoodie on the floor. His shoes beside the front door.

Nothing was there besides him.

He shook his head to himself. Reminding himself he was being silly. Turned his back to the room and opened the bathroom door.

"You killed me."

He halted.

He slowly rotated back around so he had the entire open flat in his vision.

The rooms were covered in darkness. No movement. Nothing out of place.

It's my mind.

The only explanation.

Stop it.

He couldn't let people see him like this.

Get it together.

In a sudden jolt that overcame him like an electric shock, he grew colder. The temperature around him plummeted, and he could not only see a hint of his breath in the air, but could see it fully forming into a messy cloud.

He stepped into the room, getting colder still, placing his feet on the frosty, solid floor. The lower temperature beneath his feet hurt like a sharp ice prick. He couldn't keep them on the floor for too long, otherwise the pain would spread up his ankles, to his shins, causing an ache he couldn't deny.

"Who's there?" he asked.

His eyes darted back and forth, surveying every floor, wall, and piece of furniture with precise scrutiny.

The more he stepped into the room, the more he was forced to shiver. It was as if the temperature was dropping further still with each step. He wrapped his arms around his chest, rubbing his arms, doing all he could to stay warm. At this rate, he was going to catch a cold.

"Hello?" he tried once more.

Then he had a thought.

A thought he wouldn't normally have entertained, but with all that was happening, he decided he had to.

It took him a few moments to conjure the confidence to say it. His whole body stiffened, his lip trembling, his arms shaking.

"Is that..." he tried, failing to finish the question.

He closed his eyes.

Come on.

His body shuddered as he opened his eyes once more.

In a spurt of self-assurance, he blurted it out.

"Is that Anna?"

Almost immediately he was launched off his feet, against the door of the bathroom, forced to fall into a mess on the floor.

"You killed me!" the voice repeated, this time in an aggressive scream, filling the room with ear-piercing noise. *"You killed me! You killed me!"*

Then it stopped.

The cold slunk away like a thief in the night, and he could no longer see his breath on the air.

He was left in a painful heap, huddled in a ball, denying what had just happened, willing himself to have the guts to get up.

He tried to explain it with rational thought, with other ideas of what it could be, but every flash of logical thinking escaped him as he realised his deepest fears could potentially be being carried out in his own home.

No.
These things didn't happen to him.
It had to be his mind.
It had to be.
It had to.

20

A DOZEN PAPERS AND OPEN BOOKS LAY ON THE FLOOR AROUND Oscar. He read and read and read the same words over and over again, forcing them to sink in, ensuring he remembered them.

He had really screwed up, and he knew it.

April was nice to him about it, even defending him against Julian's outburst, but deep down, Oscar had felt the scalding words were justified. He had one role in that cleansing, and it was the same role he had repeated multiple times now – say the words that ensured the bad spirit leaves April's host body.

If they waited too long to rid her body of the entity, they could end up with an unprecedented possession to deal with. A possession of someone both he and Julian cared deeply about. And it would have been Oscar at fault.

It wasn't so much that he cared about Julian's words – though he did; that's just what he told himself. It was the fact that they were right. He could have severely let April down.

So he re-read the words, again and again, repeating them out loud.

"In the name, power, and authority of Jesus Christ, Lord

and Saviour God, Holy Ghost, do the work I need right now, as I make these proclamations. In the name, power, and authority of Jesus Christ, Lord and Saviour God, Holy Ghost, do the work I need right now, as I make these proclamations."

He knew them already. He knew them so, so well. He could recite them in his sleep.

But it was like lines in a play – you could learn them until you were blue in the face, yet when it came to actually saying them in front of a crowd and remembering them under pressure, that's when you truly falter.

A knock on the door roused him from his persistent studying. It was a rhythmic knocking he recognised as April's. He leapt to his feet with a bounce, then practically dove out of the room and toward the front door, stumbling over a stray pair of shoes as he did.

"Hey, April," he said happily, opening the door to her.

His face fell as he saw her expression.

"Hey," she responded glumly.

She walked into the house and through to the living room, where she found numerous books and papers scattered around.

"Oh, Oscar." She shook her head. "You don't need to do this."

"Yes, I do. It's important. I can't get this wrong."

"It was a stumble; you are still learning. Julian was a dick. Honestly, you don't need to worry so much."

A warm glow spread through him. It was ridiculous how any time she paid him the littlest of compliments it sent him into a state of childish joy, but it did.

"I looked at our emails earlier," April began, sitting on the edge of a seat. Oscar sat opposite her. "They haven't been checked in days."

"Who should have checked them?" Oscar asked, momentarily worried this was another thing he had screwed up.

"Julian does it. We have job offers worth thousands, and no one has replied to them."

"How strange."

It was strange. Julian was the epitome of professionalism. And especially after Julian had reacted so negatively to Oscar's screw-up, it was bizarre that he wouldn't do something as routinely important as checking the company's emails and responding to new clients.

"I'm worried, Oscar," April confessed, and Oscar could see that worry in her eyes.

"Have you tried talking to him?"

"No."

"Try it. FaceTime him now. I'll be here."

"Will you hold my hand?"

Oscar's heart raced. His belly tingled.

"Of course."

April took out her phone and opened FaceTime. She held Oscar's hand tightly as she waited for Julian's response to her call.

Even though he knew it was for comfort rather than romance – or so he assumed – it still brought him great pleasure to have her skin resting against his. It occurred to him how besotted he actually was with this woman, that a simple touch of her hand could send him wild.

After an extensive wait, the call was finally answered. A few shuffles came out of the phone's speaker, rustles against a set of dirty bed sheets. Eventually, Julian's face appeared on the screen. His eyeballs were bloodshot, with pronounced bags under his eyes. His eyelids rested heavily, his face was pale, and his lips were cracked and bleeding.

April had to stifle a gasp at his appearance. Oscar had never seen him like this, and was sure she hadn't either.

"April?" Julian grunted sleepily. "What do you want?"

"What are you doing in bed, Julian? It's the middle of the afternoon."

Julian turned his head groggily toward a crack in the curtains, noticing a bright light shining through. He turned his head back, slowly and with much effort.

"What do you want, April?" he repeated.

"No one's checked the company email."

Julian sighed, running a grubby hand through his sweaty hair.

"Right. I'll do it. Is there anything else?"

Oscar knew April was trying to disguise her upset, but it was clear for him to see. Julian had taken care of her for so long, he was like an older brother – and here he was, being short and ill-tempered with her, and it was clearly breaking her heart.

"What is going on, Julian?" she persisted. "This isn't like you."

"What's not like me?"

"Have you looked in a mirror? You look like hell."

"Thanks, April," he sarcastically retorted. "Is there anything else?"

She closed her eyes and took a moment to gather herself.

"Yes. I'm worried about you."

"Well, you don't need to be."

"Really? Julian, I've never seen you like this, I–"

"Is that all, April? Because I really don't have time for this."

Her eyes watered, but she did all she could to keep it together.

"You don't have time for me?"

With an exasperated huff, Julian's face disappeared off-screen as the call ended.

April turned to Oscar, stumped, her mouth wide open in shock, fumbling for the words.

"I–" was all that she managed.

She closed her eyes and rested her head against Oscar's chest.

Oscar put a hand on the back of her head and gently stroked her hair. He tried to think of something to say, but couldn't.

So he did his best to be there for her, however little that may matter.

21

The flat had never been such a mess.

Julian didn't care.

He lay on the floor of the living room, staring at the ceiling above, motionless, unmoved. If he stayed still, maybe it would leave him alone.

Please.

Maybe *she* would leave him alone.

Was it Anna? Was it her ghost? Or was it someone with knowledge of Anna tormenting him?

Was it even paranormal?

It was more likely to be the ravings of a tired, paranoid mind. The abyss he was sinking into was consuming him into a rabid psychosis. Fragments of his mind breaking like pieces of glass entwined with painful memories he couldn't escape.

Fragments.

This is how it starts, after all. The descent into madness.

Voices. Delusions. Obsession.

Stop it.

He coughed at the stench of his own body odour. His trousers were becoming crunchy, stuck to his legs with dry sweat. Papers, magazines, and unopened mail were scattered across various parts of the floor. His furniture was out of place, his Wi-Fi box was flickering red, and his curtains kept the overpowering light out.

He closed his eyes, watching the imprint of a strip of light visible through a crack in his curtains turn into a splodge upon his retina, circling and fading into nothing.

He stretched his arms out.

Damn, my muscles ache.

His biceps felt stretched and unused.

His hand felt...

What's that?

Something was in his hand.

Something.

His hand.

It was in...

Something soft. Something bumpy yet smooth. Something small.

What could...

He lifted his hand up and squinted at the object before him.

A scrunchie.

A little girl's scrunchie. It was a reddish pink, small enough to fit at the top of a pony tail in the hair of a twelve-year-old girl.

"How did that get here..." he muttered.

He stared at it, turning it in his hands.

Unless...

Was this Anna's?

Not possible.

This is ridiculous.

Ridiculous.

She's dead.

How could she...

He leapt to his feet, determined not to believe it, focusing on channelling his thoughts into the rational.

Maybe it was April's.

Yeah, that's right. It could be April's.

Except that, in the entire time Julian had known April, he had never seen her hair tied back with a scrunchie.

No.

It's April's.

Not Anna's.

Not Anna's.

Please, not Anna's.

His head shook, flickering splashes of grease against the wall.

Please.

He refused to believe it.

No. Not real.

I can't let this be true.

He traipsed toward the kitchen, finding his throat parched and dry, desperate for water. He flung open the cupboard and clumsily withdrew a glass, hitting it against all the other glasses in the cupboard, then turned the tap on too fast and overflowed the glass.

He turned, leant against the sink, and drank the water.

He stared at the fridge.

There was something else.

The fridge...

Something on the fridge.

There was something.

What?

He placed the glass heavily on the side and approached.

Something...

A picture. Attached with a magnet to the door of his fridge.

A picture.

A picture of...

He recoiled in horror. He couldn't deny this, he couldn't. He couldn't explain it. He couldn't...

He screamed.

It wasn't her. It wasn't her. It couldn't be her.

He grabbed the picture from the front of the fridge, gawping at it.

Anna and her mother. Arms around each other. Smiling wildly, in some sunny climate, likely on holiday. Happy. Together.

Alive.

"What the fuck..."

No.

No, no, no. This is crazy. Bloody crazy.

He ripped the picture up, vigorously shaking his head, refusing.

"No, not a chance, not real, you can't, no..."

Anna.

It wasn't.

She wasn't...

He threw it in the bin and charged through the living room, back and forth, back and forth, hands in his hair, pacing back and forth, back and forth, shaking his head, refusing to believe, back and forth.

"No, no, no, it's not real, it's–"

He stopped.

The wall.

No.

He fell to his knees. Tears streamed down his cheeks like tumultuous waves.

The wall.

He couldn't deny this.

"No!" he bellowed, turning away, then looking back.

The whole of the wall was taken up with three clear words written in red.

You did this.

22

A FRANTIC COMMOTION AWOKE DEREK FROM HIS RESTLESS SLEEP. The bright light through the cell window told him it was morning.

He leant up, wearily rubbing his eyes, slowly readjusting after another night of disturbed sleep.

Cries and shouts sounded throughout the wing. At first, Derek thought a riot was underway, but as he listened to the shouts, he concluded that it must be something more.

"Leave him alone!"

"Dirty fucking warden!"

"You're next, prick!"

Derek dragged himself to his feet and edged toward the door to his cell. Normally by now, he would have been awoken by the prison officer. His cell door would have been opened, and people would be roaming freely throughout the wing.

No such thing had happened.

As he peered out of his door and down the narrow angle of the wall of cells, he couldn't see anyone else at their cell door.

So what was all the uproar about?

He turned, edging toward the window of the cell, and stood on the rim of the toilet so he could peer out of it. Climbing onto it took a few attempts, such was the pain in his bad leg, but he managed. And as the view out of his cell window became clear, shock overcame him.

Below was the courtyard of the prison, a solid cement floor surrounded by dark-red, mossy bricks. In the middle of the courtyard stood Jackson Kullins, the prison governor, feet shoulder-width apart, a stubborn frown over a piercing set of sadistic eyes.

But that wasn't what everyone was shouting at.

At the far side of the courtyard, a small set of stairs were placed against a wall; a wall as faded, graffitied, and weathered as every other wall of the courtyard. Beside this stood a masked man, fixing a rope to an arched wooden frame before him.

Derek's heart raced and his muscles stiffened.

It was the gallows.

And the man with the mask was the executioner.

Two other prison officers carried a handcuffed man, kicking and screaming toward the set of stairs. They forcibly fixed a brown bag around his head, tying it with a tight piece of string.

"Leave him alone, you piece of shit!"

"Do this, you'll be next!"

"Leave him the fuck alone!"

Helpless shouts of aggressive jeers continued to pour out of cell windows, from each floor of Derek's wing and the cells on the other sides of the courtyard. Yet, however much the abuse continued to rain down upon the scene below, it did nothing to deter the resolve upon the face of Kullins, the executioner, or the officers wrestling the man up the small set of stairs.

They placed the flailing man's head through the noose.

"Prisoner," the governor bellowed, leering at the man. "Do you have anything to say?"

The man stopped fighting. He remained still, heavy breathing causing the bag to retract.

"Very well," Kullins continued. "Hang him!"

The man was pushed off the stairs and forced to hang helplessly on the rope.

Derek watched in horror as the man's body powerlessly struggled against the suffocation of his throat. The man thrashed out his legs, pulled against his restrained hands, even tried to swing the rope back and forth with such despairing aggression Derek thought the gallows would collapse.

Then the man stopped struggling.

He just convulsed. Spasmed, his body throbbing as it struggled for oxygen.

Finally, it went limp.

It just hung there.

Dangling helplessly. The swinging to and fro calming until the empty body hung still.

Derek couldn't understand.

This was modern Britain. This was 2017.

They didn't hang people anymore.

Not for over half a century, at least.

So how was this happening? How was the governor getting away with this?

"*Silence!*" Kullins's strong voice bellowed, reverberating against the walls of the courtyard.

Every jeer and heckle ceased with instant obedience.

Every murderer, attacker, torturer – every dangerous prisoner's mouth shut firmly and abruptly. There must have been hundreds of heckling voices that instantly terminated. Their terrified eyes gazed upon the governor standing beside the loose body of the deceased.

"You see this?" the governor shouted. His voice was so

powerful it carried through the courtyard to every wing without a hint of breakage or quiver. "You continue to be miscreants, you continue to shout and holler with the audacity you have just shown, this will be *your* fate."

Derek peered at the faces at the windows of the other cells. These hardened men turned to little boys, gawking vulnerably at the man shouting from beneath them.

"I will not tolerate disobedience in my prison. Go back to your cells!"

He strode across the courtyard and disappeared past the wall.

Every face watched in ear-splitting silence as the executioner presented a pair of sheers and used it to cut the rope, forcing the dead man's body to fall into a heavy lump.

The two prison officers took an arm each and dragged the man away, disappearing out of sight, assumingly to bury the corpse in an unmarked grave.

Derek slipped from his precarious perch upon the toilet and collapsed on the floor. He winced in agony at the pounding of the solid floor against his troubled leg, but daren't make any sound.

He held the leg tightly in his arms, scrunching his face, enduring it, waiting for the pain to pass.

He did not want to make a noise.

He did not want to attract attention.

He did not want to face that man's fate.

As he sat, rocking back and forth, gripping his leg between his hands, he thought about what the apparition had told him yesterday.

The prison governor was the one they needed to look out for. Which was strange, as he appeared to be a brutal psychopath, yet had shown no supernatural element to him that Derek had seen.

The thoughts escaped as an incurable pain in his bad leg took over, but he willed himself to keep wincing in silence.

He could not let anyone hear him.

He could not risk suffering the same fate as that man.

For if the other inmates didn't kill him, if a paranormal attack didn't kill him – then there was still a far more dangerous threat looming within these prison walls.

THEN

23

SHIFTING UNCOMFORTABLY ON THE WOODEN SEAT, JULIAN peered into the distance to see if he could spot Derek. Through the crowds of people, he could just about make out the back of a tidy parted haircut, obscured by dozens of heads.

Anna's family was in there somewhere – but most of the people sat between him and Derek were nothing more than voyeurs. Vultures. Courtroom drama enthusiasts. Either the press or people who are too nosy for their own good.

Julian had intentionally taken a seat at the back, as he didn't want Derek to see him. Derek wouldn't have wanted him there. Derek was a strong man, and the most common flaw of a strong man was that they never wanted people to see them in their darkest moments.

But sometimes, the strongest people we know can be so because we see them at their most vulnerable.

Derek had always taught Julian that if you want to measure where a man is, you need to see how far they've come.

"The biggest obstacle you ever have to overcome, is your-self," Derek had once told him. Those were ten words that had been permanently engrained in his thoughts ever since.

Julian wondered, for a fleeting moment, whether he should have sat closer to the front; that way, when Derek did glance back, he would see a supportive face amongst the crowd of people who had already assumed his guilt. Maybe, in his darkest moment, Derek would wish that he had asked his dearest friend to attend.

But then again, Derek never glanced back.

He never gave his audience the pleasure of seeing his eyes break.

Julian had endured the whole ordeal with a visage of utter disdain. He'd barely been able to listen as the prosecution had ripped Derek to shreds, exposed his many heroic acts from the 1980s onwards as ravings of a dangerous, deluded fool. Each time Derek had disposed of a demon from a helpless victim, it had been turned into a disgusting, volatile, neglectful act of a delusional man.

It was a shame people made such strong assumptions about what they didn't understand.

As a result, Julian's faith in the judicial system had severely wavered, to the point where he no longer had any faith in society's ability to act with fair justice. He'd always thought of the United Kingdom as a developed country, a country of tolerance. Yet he had sat for weeks as overpaid hypocrites tore Derek's character apart in front of twelve supposedly impartial jurors.

What gave those twelve people the right to judge?

They had no special qualifications. No educated ability to scrutinise the situation with clarity.

They were being fed facts in a biased way, intended to cloud their minds until the innocent man doesn't prevail, but the best-made argument wins.

Derek was an educated man of a modest estate. His representation wasn't equal to that of the deceased girl's rich family.

The one thing Julian couldn't understand is how anyone,

whatever their beliefs, could judge Derek Lansdale as ever having anything but that girl's best interests at heart.

Her death was a tragedy, but if it weren't for Derek, it would have happened sooner and with far more violent means.

"Derek Lansdale, please rise," commanded the judge.

Derek obeyed, as did his lawyer.

Now Julian could see him.

Now Julian could see Derek's face from the side on, staring across the courtroom at the jurors. Everyone else would see his expression as assured and resilient. Julian knew him well enough to recognise the look in his eyes as a performance.

It was a look of pure fear masked by self-assurance.

Maybe Derek didn't realise how judgemental these people were. Derek probably still had faith in the system. Julian did not.

That was one thing Julian admired in Derek, whilst also resenting – the ability to see the good in everything and everyone, no matter what the situation.

"Have you reached a verdict?" the judge asked the jury's representative, who was also standing.

"Yes, we have, Your Honour," the man in a cheap grey suit replied.

"And what say you?"

"We, the jury, find the defendant – guilty – of manslaughter by gross negligence."

Derek's face didn't falter. A flicker of his cheek signalled to Julian a weakness in his eyes, like he was fighting tears, but to everyone else, he was stone cold.

Anna's mother turned to her husband, burying her head in his shoulder and weeping.

Fool.

You never want to insult a grieving mother, but Julian couldn't help but place blame on her. She approved the exorcism on her daughter. In fact, she had decided to seek Derek out and specifically request that he perform it. If Derek was responsible for the girl's death – which Julian unequivocally believed he wasn't – then she should be equally guilty.

"Mr Lansdale, have you anything to say?" the judge requested.

Derek's face slowly turned to the voyeurs watching him from the gallery, and his eyes fixed on Julian.

Julian froze.

Derek knew Julian was there.

He'd probably known all along. Of course he had. Derek misses nothing.

They held eye contact for a moment, a look of painful resolve shared between them. Derek shook his head with a fractional movement – something Julian took as an indication that they weren't to fight this; that they were to accept it and move on with their lives.

"My client does not wish to say anything," Derek's lawyer announced, "but I wish to remind you that, at the beginning of the trial, my client requested that if he was found guilty, that he be sentenced immediately."

The judge took a moment to contemplate this.

"Very well," he decided. "Derek Lansdale, you are sentenced to a minimum of fourteen years for the death of Anna Bennett through manslaughter by gross negligence. The court is adjourned."

Derek stood sternly, allowing his hands to be restrained behind his back.

Julian couldn't fight back his tears as he watched the spectators from the galleries cheering at Derek's sentence – clapping and whooping as he was unfairly found guilty of the neglectful death of a little girl under his protection.

Derek had done everything he could to save that girl from the demon.

Julian had watched, learnt, and soaked up every piece of

wisdom he could from this man. Now he was forced to watch as an officer restrained him and took him out of the courtroom to cheers and jeers.

He remained the only person sitting. Frantically immobile. Manically unsure. Devastation soaking his thoughts.

His arms shook.

His lip trembled.

Derek had disappeared behind the crowd of mocking celebrations.

He was left to sit there and think about what it all meant.

NOW

24

Jason had delayed and delayed this visit as much as possible. Over the past few days, he had exhausted the various possibilities for the doctor's death.

Suicide.

A killer who was slick enough to remove his DNA.

And leave no footprints.

And not be seen on CCTV, neither entering nor leaving the office.

He hated it, but it was time to start entertaining other options. He hated it, as he knew how others saw him. They saw him as the man who sought out the strange cases, the ones that would lead him down a path the other officers either saw as too dangerous, or, in most cases, too silly.

Being honest with himself, a year or so ago he'd have thought the exact same thing. He'd have demanded he left the station and seek psychiatric help, accompanied by a suspension.

But he had found results. Or, more pertinently, the Sensitives had found results, and he had taken credit for it. And that was the only reason he hadn't been completely dismissed. The few times he'd used the Sensitives over the last few months, he had managed to give the families involved the closure other officers couldn't.

Now he was going one step further. This wasn't just a phone call that the other officers could pretend to ignore. This was him going to Julian, asking for his help, and inviting him to come aboard a complicated murder case.

To say he felt nervous would be an understatement. He felt apprehensive, self-critical, and worried about what others were going to say about him, whether it be to his face or behind his back.

He already heard the whispers.

His colleagues thought he didn't, but he did.

He went to place a firm knock on Julian's door to find that it was already slightly ajar.

He nudged it with his hand, allowing it to creak open, and took in the dark, chaotically messy flat displayed before him.

Writing decorated the wall in red ink, ripped paper was strewn all over the floor, and the stench of body odour and expired food overwhelmed his sense of smell.

"Julian?" he asked.

A sudden gasp drew his attention.

The eyes of a man appeared from behind the sofa. It was Julian all right, but not as he had seen him before. His hair was a greasy mess, his eyes were wide and bloodshot, and he wore nothing but stained, ripped pyjama trousers. And the way Julian looked at Jason was like that of a startled wild animal.

"Julian, what the hell?" Jason asked, remaining in the doorway, wary about entering further.

"Have you come for her?" Julian asked in a quick whisper.

"Come for who, Julian? What is going on?"

Julian's eyes darted back and forth. He jumped across the floor like a demented deer, as if he had heard something, alerted to danger, hiding behind a torn armchair.

"Julian?" Jason prompted. "What are you doing?"

"You need to leave!"

"Funnily enough, I actually came to you for help."

"Help?" Julian answered with a mild roar coming from his throat. "You need to go."

"Julian, I–"

"Go!"

Jason shook his head. It was no good. He wasn't about to wait around for this.

He shut the door behind him and left.

2 5

ANOTHER CAFÉ. ANOTHER AWKWARD SILENCE AS OSCAR LOOSELY stirred his tea and April sat opposite him, waiting for him to say what they were both waiting for him to say.

Except, she seemed to be growing increasingly unsure with every attempt Oscar made at broaching the subject of his feelings for her.

He watched her for a few moments. Her eyes glazed over as she stared at the hot chocolate before her.

Normally, she would be scooping the marshmallows with her spoon, slurping on the cream, then relishing the taste of the warmth sliding down her throat.

But she wasn't.

Her mind was elsewhere.

"April, I–" Oscar tried, willing himself to tell her how he felt.

But she didn't look up, didn't respond, didn't look with waiting eyes for him to finally confess his adoration for her.

Her eyes remained down, a glum expression taking over her face.

"April, what's up?" Oscar asked, deciding that he needed to figure out her mood first.

She shrugged.

"Seriously, what is it?"

April gave a big, heavy sigh, and shrugged her shoulders again.

"You can shrug all you want, I can tell there's something on your mind."

She glanced up at him, held his eye contact for a moment, then dropped her gaze back toward her hot chocolate, watching the cream slowly melt.

"I don't know," she exhaled.

"Yeah, you do," Oscar insisted. "What is it?"

"It's just…" She opened her mouth, struggling for the words, moving her lips to form a sentence that didn't come out.

"It's Julian, isn't it?"

Oscar knew her well enough by now to read such things. He recognised the slight twitch of her nose that indicated her feeling perturbed, and he could see the tilt in her smile that indicated a troubled mind.

He hadn't even realised he knew her that well.

It was almost as if they were already a couple.

Almost.

"April, talk to me."

She lifted her head but did not fix her gaze onto Oscar, instead choosing to stare out of the window. She watched people pass by with no idea of the true reality that lurked in the darkness of their world.

"I just… I've never seen Julian like this."

Oscar nodded.

He tried to think of what to say, what words he could possibly use that would be of some comfort. He had never particularly been the one that people would go to for advice or words of reassurance. He hadn't particularly been the person people would go to for anything. He so wanted to make everything better, to wrap his arms around her and show how much she meant to him, to exorcise the demons of her mind, to will the bad thoughts away.

But he didn't know how.

"Like what?" Oscar asked, knowing it was a stupid question, but feeling he had to say something.

"Crazy. Just – crazy. He looked a state."

"Have you ever seen him like that before?"

"No, God no. I don't think I've ever even seen him without gelled hair before." She finally turned her gaze to Oscar. "I'm scared, Oscar."

"Scared? Of what?"

"Of whatever it is going on with him. What if it's something he can't overcome? What if it's something he can't fight?"

Oscar nodded. These were all relevant questions. He just didn't have the answers. He watched her, continually struggling to find a way to quell her concerns.

"I guess all you can really do is just be there for him."

Oscar concealed a smile, pleased at the wonderful advice he had just given.

"I guess, but… what if that's not enough?"

His face dropped again. He didn't know what to say.

"Look, you saw him on FaceTime. We don't know, we haven't seen him in person."

"You're right. We should go see him."

Oscar frowned. That was not what he meant, but he could hardly argue with it now.

In truth, Julian had been an arse toward him since the day they'd met. Yet he was clearly important to April, and he knew he needed to be supportive.

"Okay, let's go," Oscar decided.

"Are you coming?"

Oscar hesitated.

"But what do we do if we can't get in?"

"I have a spare key in my car."

Oscar sighed. There was no way out of this.

"Of course."

"Oh, Oscar, you are the best!"

She took his hand in hers and stroked it, sending more tingles racing up and down his body. He dropped his head to avoid revealing a blush.

"Let's go."

"Aren't you going to finish your hot chocolate?"

April shrugged and led Oscar out. The whole way out of the café and down the street, she did not let go of his hand.

2 6

APRIL EDGED TOWARD JULIAN'S FRONT DOOR FULL OF
trepidation, taking each unsure step one at a time. Oscar
remained by her side, her hand in his, holding tightly. She
didn't know whether it was for reassurance or closeness, but
she was happy to have Oscar nearby.

She let go as they approached the door, fearing that impli-
cations of romantic involvement with Oscar may just push
Julian further over the edge. She wondered why she was so
worried about Julian's reaction to the possibility of her being
romantically involved with Oscar, but pushed the thought
aside as she knocked four audible, clear knocks upon the
door.

Nothing.

She glanced at Oscar, who looked equally as unnerved as
she did. She awaited an answer, a queasy feeling churning in
the pit of her stomach.

She put her ear to the door. Listened.

Movement. There was movement. She was sure of it.

Scurrying, maybe; a persistent, vigorous scuffle.

She pressed down on the door handle and the door creaked

open into the flat. It both surprised her and scared her to find it open.

"He never leaves his door unlocked," she whispered to Oscar, growing increasingly cautious.

She entered, followed by Oscar, and instantly halted. Her jaw dropped at what she saw. Her hands covered her mouth to quell a distinct gasp.

"Oh, dear God," she whispered.

Julian was on his hands and knees, wearing nothing but stained pyjama trousers, fervently scrubbing the walls with a dirty sponge and a filthy tub of water. Smeared across the wall was a large red smudge, dripping downwards.

Her first thoughts were that the red smeared across the wall was blood, but as she apprehensively edged forward, it became clear that it was ink. Julian barely acknowledged her, continuously scrubbing, only to make the ink more and more smudged.

"Julian?" she spoke, quieter than she'd intended, still stuck in a mixture of shock and worry.

"Got to scrub it off," Julian muttered. "Got to keep scrubbing, can't talk."

"Julian?"

"Scrubbing. Anna. Got to – got to scrub."

"Julian, what are you on?" April asked, this time with a lot more force.

Julian shook his head with a few uneven shakes, his arms nervously quivering. His head continued to shake with a stuttering vibration as he persistently and aggressively scoured the wall.

"Julian, please stop!" April pleaded, trying to force a confidence to her voice, but finding it quivering with nothing but shaken anxiety.

"Can't stop…" Julian whispered.

In a spurt of frustration, April stepped forward and grabbed onto Julian's wrists, holding him still and looking him in the eyes.

The man who looked back faintly resembled Julian. His eyes were wide, bloodshot, above pronounced grey bags. They were Julian's eyes, but like she had never seen before – they were like a startled, famished creature who had no idea what was happening.

"Julian, what are you doing?"

He shook his hands, trying to release them from her grasp, but she held on more tightly.

"Julian, I'm really worried," she persisted, tears appearing in the corners of her eyes. "Please, please tell me what is happening."

"April…" he whispered, putting a pinch of hope in her mind as he recognised her. His eyes remained wide, as if in a state of permanent perplexity. "You need to go."

"Julian, please, would you–"

"Get off me!" he screamed in her face and shoved her away.

Oscar quickly intervened to catch her as she fell. She remained on the floor in his arms, watching Julian in disbelief.

He'd pushed her.

He actually pushed me…

Julian continued scrubbing, undeterred.

"Anna. Got to… Scrub. Anna. Scrub."

He didn't even register what he had done.

"Julian, what – please, tell me what to do."

"I'm fine!" he barked.

"Julian, please…"

Julian rose to his feet and turned around with a menacing glare, jabbing his finger antagonistically toward April.

"Go!" he demanded with unsettling force in his furiously shaking voice. "I got to – I got to do this – you go!"

"Let me help–"

"*Now!*"

He turned back to the wall, unsuccessfully washing away the red stains that would not fade. He scrubbed, and scrubbed, and scrubbed. Repetitively scouring at the wall with vigorous swipes, having no success of being rid of the red, but relentlessly persisting nonetheless.

"Come on, April," Oscar's soft voice spoke into her ear. "We need to go."

"I can't..." April muttered, her eyes fixed on her dearest friend in his catatonic, demented state.

"We aren't needed here," Oscar told her.

He kept his arms around her as he helped her to her feet and, with her eyes remaining on Julian, he guided her out of the flat.

Julian didn't even notice.

He barely even blinked.

OSCAR WATCHED APRIL CAREFULLY THROUGHOUT THE SOLEMN walk home, desperately wishing he could think of the right words to say.

What could you say?

Oscar already knew that he was socially awkward and rarely said the right thing at the right time, and was very much aware that whatever came out of his mouth would likely do more harm than good.

So he remained quiet, just trying to be there for her. He plucked up the courage to put an arm around her, and she not only allowed it, but rested her head in the curve of his shoulder. He pulled her closer and they walked home in comfortable silence, both relishing the closeness.

Eventually, they arrived at April's front door.

"I don't suppose you want me to come in?" he asked.

"Not today," she replied, fiddling with her keys, staring at the ground.

"I figured. Probably not the best time…" his voice drifted off into a mumble as he shifted his weight from leg to leg, unsure why he was delaying leaving.

"Thank you," she sombrely spoke.

"For what?"

"For being there for me today. You're a good friend."

A friend.

Right.

That's all he was. A good friend.

Stop it, this isn't about me. I just need to be there for her right now, it isn't the right time.

With a sad but heart-meltingly sweet smile, she leant forward and placed a delicate kiss on his cheek. Before he could respond or react, she had opened the door, said goodbye, and locked it behind her.

He stood there, staring at the door, not wanting to leave but knowing that he must.

"You're welcome, April," he spoke irritably to himself. "You're welcome, and you are oh, so perfect, and I am such a loser. I..."

She couldn't hear him. Why not now?

"I adore you. I'm crazy about you. I think you're the best person I've ever met. You make me tingle, make me nervous, and I..."

He bowed his head.

Let out a large breath of frustration.

"And I'm a loser who can't even tell you the truth about how I feel."

He turned, folded his arms, and trod heavily away. He looked over his shoulder as he left and saw April watching him from between the curtains in the front window.

He paused.

Looked at her.

She looked back.

Time to grow up.

He broke eye contact and trudged away.

Grey clouds travelled overhead and a fine rain began to

pour. Oscar let it. Allowed it to soak him from head to toe with its heavy droplets.

Julian.

What does she see in him?

He's good at what he does, but Oscar had never seen the guy crack a joke, or even smile. From day one he had been the thorn in Oscar's side, spoiling everything.

Maybe it was time Oscar gave him a piece of his mind.

If something is going on, get a grip. Get medication, get therapy, get a lobotomy if it helps – but stop April from feeling like utter shit because of it.

Yes.

That's what I'll do.

In that moment, he decided – he would confront Julian. Return to his flat and see what he could do to talk some sense into him.

Either he could help him, or tell him to get a grip and stop hurting those who care about him.

Man to man.

Or quivering boy to having-a-mental-breakdown-man.

Either way, this couldn't continue.

THEN

28

THE STREETS WERE A COLD PLACE, EVEN IN WINTER. WHEN
night set in, April was repeatedly forced to huddle in that doorway, wrapping her arms around herself, cuddling her body for
warmth. The more she rubbed her hands up and down her
chest, the more it became bearable.

Not that it was, in any way, the least bit bearable.

But there were two options. The streets, or her mum's
house.

She knew which one she'd prefer.

Not that she wasn't tempted. Nights of being abused by
drunks, urinated on by drug addicts, and propositioned for
prostitution by perverts who thought she was that desperate –
those were the nights she thought about how warm the room
back at her mum's house was.

But that room had probably been the only warmth in that
house.

They had probably turned it into a home gym by now. Or,
in all likelihood, a bar, with shelves of spirits and fridges of
beer they could use to get themselves nicely drunk and aptly
abusive.

She leant her head back and closed her eyes. Tried to sleep. She never slept properly, not on the streets – you always had to be ready and alert. Some scumbag may come to rob you or touch you up, and you had to be ready to react, however tired you may be.

"April," came a voice nearby.

She promptly turned her head to find a large figure silhouetted by the lamppost behind it, standing over her.

This person knew her name.

Oh, God, was it her mum? Was it her mum's boyfriend? Had they found her?

"April, it's okay," the voice repeated. It wasn't a voice she recognised. It was well spoken, like the lead in a romantic comedy.

She didn't know anyone who spoke like that.

"How do you know my name?" she demanded.

The figure crouched beside her. As his face came into view, it surprised her how young this man looked. He couldn't be any more than late twenties. He was clean-shaven, with dark-blond hair swept to the side, and wearing smart trousers with a shirt and an open collar.

"Because I've seen you," he answered with an air of obtrusive charm about his voice.

"How have you seen me? You been following me?"

"No, no," he chuckled. "I've never met you before tonight. I meant that I've seen you in my mind."

Oh great, another drug addict.

She clenched her fists, ready to defend herself.

"Back off, arsehole, before I break your jaw," she threatened.

"Whoa, April, I'm not here to hurt you," he insisted. "Quite the opposite. My name is Julian."

Julian?

Was this some toffy private school boy come to taunt her?

Well, she was having none of it.

146

"Fuck off, Julian. I mean it."

"I have a gift," he told her, ignoring her protests. "A special gift. A gift that means I can sense other people like me. They are called Sensitives. That's what you are, April. You are a Sensitive."

What was this guy on?

"I don't know what you want from me, mate – but you ain't getting it!"

"Tell me, April, have you ever seen something you knew was there but couldn't be? Have you ever made something happen that you couldn't make happen, yet still did? Have you had a feeling that something was with you, but something you couldn't explain in words?"

She paused, peering at him, curiously cautious. Every word he said made sense, and she knew exactly what he was talking about. But it was too close, too bizarrely accurate. How could he know about these things?

"I know because I am the same," he told her, immediately answering her thoughts. "And this isn't a curse you've been given. Quite the opposite, in fact. And I'm here to show you how to use it, how to harness it."

Could she harness it?

All these things she saw, she did, she felt – he could teach her to use it?

To give it a purpose?

"Who are you?" she asked, her layer of thick skin thinning.

"Like I said, my name is Julian, and I am a Sensitive, like you, ready to show you the way."

He stood and held out his hand.

"What do you say, April? Want to come with me? Want to find out what you can do?" He looked over his shoulder, and up and down the street. "Or do you want to stay here, eating scraps and sleeping with one eye open every night?"

She took his hand.

She knew exactly which option she wanted.

NOW

29

DEREK SAT ON THE EDGE OF THE BED, SURVEYING THE MEDICAL room with curiosity. It was, without a doubt, the most cheerful room of the prison, with charts and posters about the human body decorating its light-blue walls.

Jane, the prison's doctor, sat before him, nursing his leg in her delicate hands. She was in her early thirties, with long, blond hair, and a smile that was always eager to welcome him. She was also the only person he'd found within the prison that could engage him in intellectual conversation, and visiting her had often been a welcome relief, despite it being for his deteriorating health.

"Just stretch it for me," she instructed him. He attempted to follow her instructions but winced at the pain before he could fully straighten his knee.

"That's okay," she reassured him, allowing him to move his leg back as she made a few notes on a pad. "Lift up your shirt for me."

She placed the end of her stethoscope against Derek's chest, prompting him to flinch from the cold of the metal against his skin.

"Been reading much more Hawkins recently?" she asked.

"Just finished *The Grand Design*. Found it fascinating."

"Really?"

She paused as she listened through her stethoscope, as though stopping at a moment of concern. She placed it back around her neck before making a few more notes.

"What's the matter, Doctor?" Derek inquired. "You don't look happy."

"I'm concerned, Derek, if I'm to be honest with you."

"Why?"

She hesitated, fiddling with the pen in her mouth, brushing her long, blond hair back over her shoulder. Derek wondered how tough it must be being an attractive woman working in a prison, and that she must get many taunts and comments from the more hormonal convicts. She seemed a strong person, and if it deterred her, you couldn't tell.

"Your heart rate is down, your blood pressure is down, and you can't straighten your leg."

"Is that bad?"

"Well, you could straighten it a few weeks ago. And if I was to put your heart rate over the past few months into a graph, it would have a negative correlation."

"Oh."

She sighed. Derek watched her as she puzzled something through her mind, her thoughts entwining as she struggled to verbalise the sad repercussions of Derek's deteriorating health.

"Just tell me straight," Derek requested. "Just be honest with me."

"Okay, Derek." She nodded and turned to him, forcing a sad, sympathetic smile. "You aren't in a good way. And I think you know that. And I think you know why."

Derek's eyes dropped.

At this rate, he would never see the outside of the prison again.

At this rate, those prison walls would be the last thing he saw.

"I understand."

"I'm going to see you again in a few days, I think, maybe prepare a few tests, see where we can go from here. Get you some treatment. Okay?"

"Thank you, Doctor."

"Take care of yourself, Derek."

Derek stood, resting his weight on his good leg, reaching for his walking stick. He used it to hobble forward, taking far longer to reach the door to the doctor's office than he had done a month, or even a week ago.

He placed a hand on the door handle and turned it.

It wouldn't turn.

He tried again, forcing his feeble strength against it. It must be locked.

"The door's locked," Derek announced, and turned back to the room.

Jane was gone.

She wasn't there.

In fact, no one was there.

"What's with the–"

There was nothing.

Not even equipment. The room was empty.

What on earth...

He tried the door again. It wouldn't open. It was definitely locked.

He turned back to the empty room.

There was no bed, no equipment, no Jane. It was empty, as if it was a vacant storage room, absent of life.

Derek couldn't understand it. He frantically shook his head, his arms shaking in fear.

Had he just imagined it?

Had he just hallucinated the entire events of the last ten minutes?

It wasn't possible.

It wasn't.

It...

"Jane?" Derek whispered.

An eerie wind brushed against him, stinking of rotten meat.

He turned and pushed down on the door handle with all his force. It opened, forcing him to barge through.

As he steadied himself, he looked up. He filled with dread. Shaking, as he cast his eyes over the stern, hostile face of the prison governor.

"What are you doing?" Kullins demanded.

"The door was locked. Thank you for opening it."

"What are you on about, you fool? There is no lock."

Derek's eyes shot to the door handle.

There was no place for a key. No latch. Nothing.

How could that be?

What is happening?

The governor stepped into Derek's personal space, looming over him with a severe advantage in build and height, narrowing his eyes into a menacing glare.

"Are we going to have a problem?" the governor asked in a slow, hushed voice.

"No, sir," Derek answered, his lip trembling, his weak bones shaking, his feeble knees battering against each other.

"Get back to your cell."

"Yes, sir."

Derek turned as swiftly as his frail body would allow and stumbled forward, shuffling as quickly as he could, but nowhere near as quick as he once was.

He did not look back; but for the entirety of his long walk back to A Wing, he could still feel the governor's dirty breath breathing down his collar.

3 0

Oscar charged up the path to the door of Julian's flat, full of fury, full of all the words he planned to hurl Julian's way.

How dare he upset April like this!

You need to get a grip!

What do you think you are doing?

Each of those words fell away once he actually placed his hand on the handle and realised it was time to say them all.

It was Julian. He was like an older brother who bullied you, yet you still craved his approval. Oscar hovered, feeling a wave of nerves overcome him, nearly succumbing to the cowardice he had become most acquainted with.

Come on, man. For once in your life, just... have some guts!

Willing himself on, he leant on the door and barged into the flat.

"Julian, I don't know what you think you are doing–"

Julian wasn't there.

Oscar scanned the room, searching for him.

The ink still covered the wall in a light-red coating, like a thin layer of watercolour paint.

But Julian...

Oscar stepped forward, looking in the bedroom, the kitchen, then, as he stepped into the living room, he tripped over something heavy, sprawled across the floor.

Julian was laid flat out on his back, his eyes open, staring wide-eyed with a fixed gaze upon the ceiling above.

"Julian?" Oscar asked, surprised by Julian's catatonic state.

Julian didn't reply. His eyes rigidly open. His mouth agape.

His face not showing a flinch of reaction.

"Julian, come on, we're getting sick of this, man."

Julian still didn't reply.

He just stared at the nothingness floating above him. Alert, wide eyes, fixed upon a stationary head upon a solidly immobile body. He was like a plank, stiff and unmoving, laid stubbornly on the floorboards.

"Julian, I think it's time–"

Julian muttered something. Something so quiet Oscar couldn't make it out. Julian's lips only budged a fraction, as the rest of his body remained immobile.

"Julian–"

"She never leaves..." Julian uttered once more.

"Who, Julian?" Oscar asked. "Who never leaves?"

"She's here... She's always here..."

Oscar knelt beside Julian. His anger had been replaced by pity. He was unsure whether to tell him to get a grip, or to get him help.

"Who, Julian? What's going on?"

"Anna..."

Anna?

She was the girl who died... The one in Julian's first exorcism...

Is that what this was all about?

"Anna's dead, Julian," Oscar told him, then instantly regretted being so direct.

"That doesn't stop her…" Julian spoke in another quiet utterance.

"Doesn't stop her what, Julian? What is she doing?"

Julian's head finally moved, but Oscar wished that it hadn't. It rotated so slowly and so sinisterly toward him that it sent chills firing up his body. Julian's chilling gaze was no longer pointed at the ceiling, but at Oscar's terrified eyes.

"She's torturing me… She won't let me go…"

"Won't let you go?"

"It has Derek, too…"

Derek? How does it have Derek? Derek was in prison. Surely if there was a haunting in prison, then Derek would know?

Unless that's what Julian and Derek had spoken about in the prison after Julian had requested a solitary audience with Derek's company.

"Julian, you need to let me understand–"

Oscar placed his hand on Julian's shoulder.

Like a bolt of lightning, he was taken off his feet and hurled across the room. He smacked into the far wall, hitting his head.

Flashes. Glimpses. They battered against his vision like blinding, white light.

He had no time to rub or nurse his injury. A devastating vision abruptly preoccupied his mind.

It felt as if his brain was pounding against his skull. A migraine overtook him, as a sense of clarity descended upon him in a deafeningly apparent glimpse.

The prison.

Gloucester Prison. Derek's home.

Crumbling.

Empty.

Vacant for years.

No one was there.

The walls were empty.

The car park was empty.

The vacant visitor's room, the solemn cells within, the corridors leading to the cells.

It was empty.

The entire prison was…

How was it empty?

Oscar looked to Julian, who remained on the floor.

Touching him had given Oscar a glimpse.

The mask had fallen.

The prison.

It was…

"Oh, shit," he gasped.

Derek was in terrible danger.

31

Oscar urged the taxi driver to go faster as he scrolled to April's number in his phone's address book.

She had implied that he shouldn't contact her, that she wished to be left alone. But that didn't matter now. He needed to talk to her with a severe urgency, and this taxi driver was tediously sticking to the speed limits.

He put the phone to his ear, listening to the ring, waiting for her to pick up.

"Hi, this is April, I can't answer the phone right now but–"

"Damn it, April."

Oscar hung up, then selected her name once more, placing the phone to his ear.

It rang and rang and rang and rang until eventually…

"Hi, this is April, I can't answer the–"

"Christ's sake, come on!" Oscar growled, unable to avoid his frustration from pouring out.

He selected her name once more. He knew she was there. If he just kept persisting and persisting, eventually she would get fed up and answer.

Surely.

"Hi?" came an irritated voice.

"April, thank God!"

"Oscar, I thought I told you I wanted to be left alone."

"Yes, I know, but – just listen, April!"

"Oscar, now's not the time."

"Would you just listen for fuck's sake!"

The line remained silent as Oscar huffed, surprising himself with his dramatic outburst.

"I had a glimpse. The prison we went to, it had a block on it, I couldn't see it. Then I touched Julian and it's the same thing that's haunting the prison that's haunting him, so that meant the block dropped, then I could see it, I could see it, April, in its true form."

"What are you on about, Oscar? See what in its true form?"

"The prison!"

Oscar realised he was stumbling over his words, being unclear, but he couldn't help it. His desperate concern was becoming stronger and stronger, growing more and more pertinent, filling his mind with terror.

"What about the prison?"

"April, I had a vision that it was empty, that it was crumbling down."

"That it was empty?"

"Yes. Then I looked it up. I looked the prison up on my phone, April."

"And what? What happened?"

Oscar ran his hand over his head, through his hair, trying to find the words, trying to force a coherent sentence to his lips.

"I looked it up, and I looked up its history, and I saw, April, I saw..."

"Saw what, Oscar?"

He knew she was getting frustrated.

He tried to calm himself down. Tried to force himself to see sense, to avoid the nonsensical ramblings.

"The prison, April – it shut in 2013. It was open, then it shut in 2013."

"What do you mean it shut in 2013?"

"April, it hasn't been a prison for four years. It's closed."

THEN

32

DEREK'S WRISTS BURNT. HE'D NEVER THOUGHT ABOUT HOW painful handcuffs would be.

He'd never really given thought to this experience whatsoever, if he was being honest with himself.

It was so surreal.

It felt as if it didn't exist. As if the police van he sat in the back of wasn't real. As if the voices of the police talking in the front were in a distant dream.

He knew that he would have to face his reality soon enough.

Because within an hour, he would be in a prison cell. Alone. In uniform. Staring at a bed and toilet in a cell smaller than a child's bedroom. With nothing but him and his guilt to fill the walls around him.

Prison. That's where they said he was being taken.

Prison.

It was actually happening.

Just as the thought entered his mind, the police van stopped.

Then... nothing.

Nothing happened.

The voices of the officers were no longer there. In fact, he could no longer see their shadows against the blackened glass that separated him from them. He wished he had a window he could peer out of; that he could use to gain some clarity over what was happening, but he had to settle for patience.

Eventually, the answers would reveal themselves.

He was left to his thoughts. Left with frantic worries spinning around and around.

What if he was attacked?

What if a prisoner took offence to him?

What if...

No.

He bowed his head and allowed the truth to settle over him.

I deserve to be here.

A girl died in his presence. Because he couldn't save her. Because he didn't do enough.

He was getting off lightly.

Her young, sweet face implanted itself in the forefront of his thoughts. He closed his eyes and allowed his troubled mind to dwell on her delicate eyes. He saw her not as she was when she died, or when she had a demon pounding against the inside of her flesh. No, he saw her in the early days of possession. When she still had her young, beautiful, smiling face. When she beamed up at him. When she greeted him with thorough politeness, eager to interact, eager to allow him into her family's home. Eager to show him around, to show him her favourite toy, her favourite song, her favourite...

No.

He was getting off lightly.

A girl was dead.

And it was his fault.

"Derek."

His eyes shot open.

His head spun around. Scanned the van.

He was alone.

His sight contested as much.

But his other senses…

The reek of rotting meat hit him with sudden impact.

He knew what that meant.

It was a smell he had grown familiar with when fighting the demonic.

"Derek," the voice boomed out once more.

"What?" Derek snarled.

"This is what God gives you now."

He frowned. He was not fooled.

"You are no God," Derek defied.

"And where is he?"

Derek did not respond. He knew better than to communicate with something attempting to enter his mind, something attempting to poison his thoughts.

"You killed her."

He ignored it.

It was right, but he ignored it.

"You may as well have put a knife to her throat and cut it yourself."

He held back tears.

He would not let it enter his head.

He would not.

He could not.

"You could have torn her scrawny face from her meek body."

"Stop it."

He grew angry with himself for responding.

"You may as well have punched yourself up her cunt like I did."

"Shut up!"

He bowed his head. Scrunched up his eyes.

He could not let it enter his head.

Because then it would involve him in whatever it wished to do.

He was guilty. He felt guilty. But the power of that guilt…

It wanted to play on his–

He closed his head, scrunched up his eyes, did all he could to block it out.

"You may as well have eaten her from the inside like I did."

"Go away!" he cried out.

Years of serving, of being an expert, of telling others to ignore the taunts, and he could not follow his own advice.

Because it was right.

He could not accept it, but it was.

He may as well have just killed her himself.

"Yes. That's it. That's right."

It was his fault.

"That's right, it is your fault."

And he had to pay.

"And you will. You will not only pay for her death, but for the hundreds of demons you have defeated, for all the times you have fought me. You will suffer."

"No!"

The backdoors to the van swung open.

And he forgot everything. Everything he had learnt about fighting the demonic. Everything he had taught others.

He couldn't think. It felt like fingers digging into his skull, taking over his mind until he couldn't think of anything but the pain.

Reality slipped away.

His mind was going elsewhere.

Somewhere else. Somewhere he would not be able to fight.

Something put a block on his mind. Stopped him from resisting. Stopped him from fighting

And he let it.

Let it wash over him.

He fell still. Silent. Submissive.

It entered him. Entered his mind like a poisonous gas penetrating his nostrils, his ears, his mouth.

It consumed him. Took to every part of his lungs, his cells, his thoughts – until it was as much a part of his veins as his blood.

A man stood in front of Derek, a cloud of smoke settling behind him. His menacing glare fixed intently on Derek's eyes.

Derek fell to the floor, cowering, his mind racked with guilt.

"My name is Kullins," the man told him – a sick, wide grin spreading across his pale face. "And it's time to come home."

NOW

33

DEREK STOOD CAUTIOUSLY ON THE WING, LOOKING BACK AND forth, back and forth.

Some prisoners were playing cards around a table, and further down the corridors, some were playing pool. He noticed a group of prisoners picking on a younger, timid inmate, surrounding their victim and bullying him into submission.

To Derek's far right was the prison officer on duty.

Doing nothing about the poor lad being bullied.

As always.

Normally, this would concern Derek. He feared what would happen if another prisoner chose to kick out his cane and show him who's boss. He tended to keep himself to himself, and that had served him well so far, but there was only so much he could do until they chose to turn their ill treatment toward him.

But today this was a relief, as Derek did not want to be noticed. And if the prison officer was not distracted by a group of thugs surrounding and pounding on an intimidated youngster, he would be unlikely to notice what Derek was doing.

He stepped back into his cell, looking around cautiously, remaining unnoticed.

The haunting had been stepping up its attacks recently; that was clear.

It meant Derek had to step up his defence.

He withdrew a few pieces of wood from beneath his bed, retreating to the corner of his cell and turning his back to the door so the items were shielded from any prying eyes passing by.

Getting a few loose pieces of wood hadn't been easy. It was bizarre, really, how if he claimed he smoked, they would hand him a lighter, or if he wanted a coffee, he would be allowed a kettle. But items such as wooden blocks that would not set alight an officer or burn another prisoner with boiling water were deemed as a banned, offensive weapon.

Maybe it's because there was no context as to why someone would want wood within a prison, therefore, it could only be used as a weapon.

Well, I am using it as a damn weapon.

Just not the same kind of weapons other prisoners may wield...

He pulled out a large piece of frayed rope, well used and worn down from parcels and transporting various items, but the best he could get.

And it would do.

It hadn't taken much to fool the corrupt system within these walls. A few packets of cigarettes to the right inmate on C Wing and he had the items he desired.

In all honesty, the prison officers likely turned away and pretended they didn't know. After all, if they came into a wing and decided to notice, it would be more trouble than it was worth. If they decided to stand up to a prisoner, they were vastly outnumbered.

He held out the two small planks of wood. The corners

were sharp, and splinters poked off the wooden slabs like a porcupine's back, but it would do.

A few small cuts from a few splinters was nothing compared to the obtrusive aggression a malevolent force could wager against him.

He laid the longer plank on the floor and placed the smaller plank sideways a third of the way down.

It made a rustic, rough, homemade cross.

He had no holy water. No rosary beads. No Bible, no prayer book, nothing else he could use to perform an exorcism or a cleansing. But he would rather be with this makeshift weapon than be left defenceless against the violent paranormal elements he could feel roaming the prison wings.

He wrapped the rope around the two shards of wood, placing it diagonally one way, then the other, then around a few more times, tightening it repeatedly until the two pieces of wood were fixed in place.

After wrapping numerous circles at various angles, he checked the security of the cross, ensuring that the two pieces of wood were firmly fastened.

They didn't budge.

He finished the cross with a final knot.

This was it.

No turning back.

This night, once everyone was asleep, once darkness had descended on these dirty, worn-out walls, he would put up his fight.

He would exorcise these demons from this prison.

He just had to put the cross somewhere.

Suddenly, it struck him.

Something had happened.

The wing. It had fallen into a dead silence.

The general ambience of prisoners talking and interacting had ceased. An uncomfortable hush had descended.

Eerie absence floated into Derek's cell. There was no idle chatter, no competitive gloats of inmates winning at cards, no leers from intimidating, aggressive bullies. Never had silent thugs made him more worried.

A few heavy footsteps grew closer, then ceased.

Derek slowly turned over his shoulder.

The dark, shadow-encased face of the prison governor stood in the doorway of his cell, his narrow-eyed glare intensifying into a brutal grimace.

"What have you got there?" Kullins asked.

3 4

Oscar's and April's eyes flickered with disbelief as they stared dumbfounded at the computer screen.

"We really need Julian for this," Oscar regretfully admitted.

"Julian is not of any help to us," April hesitantly responded. "For now, we are on our own."

"I just – I can't..." Oscar ran his hands through his hair, searching for the words. "We can't do this on our own."

"We either do it on our own, or Derek..." April trailed off.

"Derek is a powerful exorcist; surely he can manage."

"Did you see the state of him?" April closed her eyes and shook her head, wishing she could think of a better solution. "Besides, Derek has no idea how big this thing is. He probably thinks it's just a small haunting, not... a total mirage. Whatever it is has taken him over completely. He is as good as possessed."

April stood, pacing the room, racking her thoughts for a solution that was logical and unlikely to put either of them in fatal danger. Unfortunately, such ideas were not forthcoming.

Oscar sat at the computer, taking over the research, re-looking over what they had found. He willed the words he had already read numerous times to somehow change. Maybe, if he looked again, with his own eyes, his full attention on the screen, he would find that the words said something else.

He was kidding himself.

"Do you know which cell he's in?" Oscar asked.

"No, why?"

"Can you find out?"

April paused for a moment, searching the room, looking for something that would indicate Derek's cell number. There was paper work Julian had left on the side so she started sifting through it, finding a few pages with the prison's watermark on.

Reading back the opening paragraph, Oscar read what it had told them about the history of the prison.

PARANORMAL RESEARCHERS HAD FOUND *multiple occurrences of supernatural phenomena in A Wing, Cell 25. The spirit of a girl called Elizabeth, murdered in the fifteenth century on the land where the prison was later built, has been seen by prisoners and guards throughout the prison's open years. One prisoner claimed to see Elizabeth's disembodied hand pointing at him.*

"I'VE GOT IT," April said.

It can't be. It can't be. It can't be.

"What is it?" Oscar asked.

"He's on A Wing, in Cell 25."

Shit.

"Of course he bloody is."

Oscar continued to scroll downwards, reading about an infamous prison governor who had owned the prison in the late 1800s. The man had executed over a hundred prisoners and buried them in unmarked graves. What's more, this governor was thought to have possessed another prison governor in the 1990s.

"Have you read this about the governor?" Oscar asked.

"No, what does it say?"

"It says that a governor, named Jackson Kullins, marched over a hundred prisoners to the gallows and watched them being executed. Apparently, another prison governor in the 1990s marched numerous prisoners there for petty misbehaviour and tried to hang them, just as Kullins had done before. He was stopped at the last minute, at which point he couldn't remember what he had done. April, if this prison governor is still there..."

"What's the governor's name again?" April asked, lifting an old letter from Derek that she found to have mention of the prison governor.

"His name was Jackson Kullins," Oscar read.

April dropped the letter.

Oscar didn't need to ask her why.

He stood, unable to sit anymore, anxious energy in his legs forcing him to pace.

"But why?" Oscar mused. "Why would Derek allow this thing to take him?"

April sank into deep thought, then turned to Oscar with an abrupt click of her fingers.

"Guilt!"

"What?"

"The block on you dropped when you touched Julian, right?"

"Yes, but I don't get what that—"

"Don't you see? Derek was there when Anna died. His guilt... Entities thrive on negative energy. Derek must feel so bad that it's powering an entire prison!"

Oscar shook his head, at first in disbelief, then in vigorous denial.

"How the hell are we supposed to do this?" he asked, a pained expression entwining his face. "This isn't an entity. This is something powerful enough to create a whole prison full of apparitions. I can't do this. I can't even get a sodding incantation right!"

"We don't have a choice," April told him.

"This is too big an obstacle–"

April stepped forward, ceasing Oscar's nervous pacing by placing her hands on the side of his face. She brought his head in close to hers and leant her forehead against his. She was so close he could feel her breath against him. His lips were almost touching hers.

Almost.

"A good man once said," she told him, "that the biggest obstacle you have to overcome is yourself."

"Who said that?"

April smiled. Once they had gathered their things, she took his hand, and together they left.

3 5

Kullins' hardened eyes glared upon Derek with a sickening intensity. He seemed to be forever in shadow, walking around with lengthy, effortless strides, looming over his victims whatever their size. His face looked incapable of smiling. His presence alone filled a room with a negative ambience that sent fear trickling down your forehead in drops of desperate perspiration.

"Er..." Derek stuttered.

"I said," the governor repeated with a slow, quiet intensity that allowed him to pronounce each and every syllable, "what have you got there?"

Derek looked down upon the wooden cross he had so slickly fashioned moments ago. It had offered him a feeling of salvation. Now he held it in his quivering hands with an immediate feeling of dread.

"It's..." Derek thought about what excuses he could give, but found none presenting themselves. "It's a cross. It gives me comfort. It–"

Derek's voice cut off as soon as the governor took a large

stride into the cell, encompassing Derek in his shadow as he peered at the item.

"It looks like a weapon."

"It – it's not, I swear, it's just a crucifix. It gives me comfort. I needed one."

The governor held out his large hand with his thick fingers protruding from his dirty palm.

Derek didn't hesitate, understanding what this meant, handing over the cross, his hands shaking so vigorously they made the cross bounce from side to side.

The governor took the supposed weapon, scrutinising it with his eyes. He ran a finger over it, feeling the edge of the splinters without a wince of pain. He glanced at Derek, his fleeting stare indicating that the splinters were not holding Derek in good stead. Kullins' hand continued to trace the edge until they reached the end of the cross, and felt the large spike.

"Are you telling me," he directed at Derek, "that this sharp point could not do someone damage?"

"I suppose it could, but–"

"So you are about to tell me that you were not intending to use it to attack another prisoner, an officer, or even me, the governor himself?"

"No! Not at all! I swear, I never meant anyone any harm!"

The governor lowered himself to Derek's level with an unhurried, measured descent, and gave him a deadly, prolonged glare.

"Do you think I'm a fool?" he asked, in such a husky whisper only Derek could have heard him.

"No. No, I don't."

The governor nodded, as if deciding something in his mind, a dreaded conclusion being drawn without any other choice.

He stood, turned to the prison officers standing obediently behind him, and gave a nod. They entered the cell, grabbed Derek by his arms, and dragged him out.

"What? Where am I going?" Derek desperately asked.

He tried thrashing, struggling, but it did nothing. His leg wouldn't lift without pain, and his muscles were far too decrepit for him to muster the energy required.

"You have made a big mistake," the governor told Derek, then turned to the officers. "This way."

"What?" Derek panicked, overcome with fear and dread.

Where were they taking him?

The gallows?

Surely not.

They wouldn't be allowed to hang him for this. He had human rights. This was 2017; you couldn't treat people like this, not anymore. Executions hadn't been done in this country for a long, long time. Even if they were still being used, Kullins couldn't legally execute him for forging a weapon.

It was not possible.

Yet there he was, being dragged through the wing, watched helplessly by the passing, solemn faces of the other prisoners, all lined up outside their cells.

The governor was one man. There were easily seventy prisoners on that wing. Why weren't they doing anything?

The governor told the prisoners to line up and they did it. This was just one man. One man whom, if they worked as a unit, they could all easily overthrow.

But they didn't. They remained static. Terrified.

How did one man create so much fear?

This didn't make sense.

None of this made sense.

What was going on? Was this something playing a trick? A mirage? A hallucination? The onset of psychosis? Or maybe all these people were possessed?

No. Derek had never known such a thing to happen. Even when fighting in the harshest war known to man, he had never encountered a mass possession before.

So what, then?

What was happening?

The prisoners' regretful faces faded from view as he was dragged through the corridor, forced to watch the crumbling ceilings pass.

It was strange… The prison had been in such great shape. Not perfect, but liveable. And now…

Now it was crumbling. Peeling. Falling to pieces.

The paint was cracking, dropping from the walls. The cell bars were growing rust, the ceiling plaster falling apart.

What is going on?

He found himself dragged into the courtyard, feeling the harsh bumps of the pavement digging into the back of his legs as they pulled him across the rough ground, forcing him to cry out in anguish.

The officers dumped him onto the dry gravel.

Derek looked up and saw the executioner preparing a noose in the exact place he had seen a man hang only days ago.

36

ONCE AGAIN, APRIL MANAGED TO FRIGHTEN OSCAR WITH WHAT she claimed were 'impeccable' driving skills. She swung around every corner, sped through every traffic light, and overtook every car she could.

Oscar's hands gripped the side of his seat until they hurt.

"Jesus, April, let's try and be alive when we get there."

Eventually, they reached the country roads that occupied the final bulk of the journey. Oscar could see the concentration on April's face. She was intently focused as she swung around the corners, ensuring they reached the prison in one piece and in record time.

When she finally reached the prison car park, Oscar's jaw dropped.

He opened the door and edged out, taking small steps toward the prison, looking upon it with amazement.

This was nothing like the prison he had previously been to. It was the same prison. But it was...

"What?" April asked. "What is it you see?"

Oscar placed a hand on her shoulder. Being a conduit, she could then use his ability to glimpse in order to see the prison in its true form. And as the veil lifted, she too was stupefied to the spot, struck with astonishment.

The prison's sign that had once displayed itself proudly above its entrance with perfect, clean and clear lettering, was now a faded image. Its print was covered in moss, and its proud symbol speckled in mould of various shades of green and brown.

Trees leant at crooked angles, overhanging the car park. Leaves flaked from curving twigs, prickling out from corrupt, contorted roots. The ominously lavish spiralling of branches blocked out the late evening light, leaving the prison in darkness.

The thick stones that had made up the sturdy wall still stood, but were covered in blemishes and divots. Weeds entwined weeds, travelling up and around the space between the slabs. The windows had large, twisting cracks, and the path leading up to the prison was stained with tufts of overgrown grass.

"What the..." April gasped.

"How did we not see this before?"

"Oscar, for something to be able to do this... It has to be really powerful. I mean – Derek is stuck in a full spiritual realm, strong enough to create a whole delusion for both him and us as visitors."

Her lip trembled.

"And he has absolutely no idea..."

Oscar vaguely nodded, not a clue what to say. There was no verbal acknowledgement he could give that would display his anxiety at the task ahead.

"Oh my God..." April suddenly realised something. "But if this is being powered by both Derek *and* Julian's guilt, then..."

"What? What is it?"

"Julian... That's how it's this powerful..."

Oscar frowned, confused, unable to make sense of what she was saying.

"What is it, April?"

Her mouth widened even further. A sense of understanding overcame her, prompting her to shake with dread.

"Both Derek and Julian were there when Anna died. They were there when this started. They are both going to be there when it ends."

April's eyes dropped for a moment, then weakly rose to meet Oscar's.

He knew what she was about to say. And he really, truly, did not want her to say it.

"No, April, no," he refuted. "You can't."

"I have to."

"No..."

"We have to defeat it for both Julian and Derek, at the same time – or it won't work."

Oscar shook his head. There was no way he could do this on his own. This prison was being overpowered by a presence with the ability to concoct an entire world and present it to Derek, not just in images, but by interacting with him. This was a savage, eager, powerful malevolent force.

And I'm just a shitty little boy.

"Please, April..."

April stepped forward, placing her hands once more on the side of Oscar's face, pulling him in close, meeting his eyes with hers, inches away.

Whilst the same rush of excitement filled him, he was also overcome with the hard-hitting feeling of dread.

"If this thing has Julian, then he's also in incredible danger. I have to help him."

"Then we'll do it afterwards! We'll free Derek, then he can help!"

"No, Oscar, you don't get it. This thing is haunting them

both. We need to fight it at both places, otherwise it will be no good. Otherwise, we don't stand a chance."

As Oscar realised there was nothing he could do to change her mind, he savoured the moment of closeness. He put his arms around her, holding her near. He could feel her body against his, could feel her arms beneath his soft touch. He wished he could never let her out of his embrace.

He was no longer just mortified for his own safety, but for hers too.

"You'll be fine, Oscar."

"But what happened before, when I forgot the–"

"What happened before was a temporary glitch. It happens. You are stronger and more powerful than you could possibly realise. Once you realise your full strength, these things will fear you."

"Well, I'd say that day is pretty far off because right now, I'm pissing my pants."

She giggled, forcing a mystified smile in return.

"By the way," April softly spoke. "The answer is yes."

"What do you mean?"

"Yes. I do feel the same way."

With that revelation, she pulled his forehead down and placed a soft, tender kiss upon it.

She wrenched herself away without looking back, ran back to the car, and sped out of the car park.

Oscar turned and looked upon the prison.

He felt sick.

"Right," he told himself. "Time to get it together."

Feeling a surge of forced self-confidence, he charged toward the door. As soon as he reached the threshold, a large invisible force punched him in the gut with an unforgiving gust of wind, sending him flying backwards, landing on the harsh cement of the car park surface.

This was not going to be easy.

37

DEREK'S GUT CHURNED, ROLLING AND ENTWINING, AN ACIDIC feeling of nausea battling his stomach.

His eyes stuck open as he stared agape at the gallows being mounted and the noose being hung atop it. A man with a covered face – a cowardly man Derek knew was just a regular prison officer being forced into being an executioner – attached the rope securely to the wooden beam, ensuring it was fixed well enough that there was no possibility of it giving way.

So there was no way, should Derek's neck fail to snap, that he would not subsequently choke to death.

Derek looked around, searching for an escape, pleading for salvation.

He was trapped inside a large group of prison officers forming a perfect rectangle, creating an invisible box from which he could not escape. They stood in perfect symmetry and equal distance to one another. Their hands were behind their backs and their heads were partially dropped, each of their faces echoing the same blank, solemn expression.

They were almost too unified. Too perfectly coordinated. Mirroring each other too flawlessly.

It was unnatural.

Derek leapt to his feet and attempted to run, but fell onto his front. An officer went to stop him, but found they needn't, as he lay pathetically upon the floor writhing in agony from his weak body and his rotting leg.

A mouthful of sick lurched up his throat, forcing him to spew blood and lumps over the crooked cement.

A few raindrops stuttered upon the ground, falling loosely, as if an omen of things to come.

He looked up from his place on the floor, watching as Kullins climbed the stairs of the gallows to check the strength of the noose.

The man lifted out an arm and placed a rough fist around the rope. With a sadistic smile he tested it, confirming its secure rigidity. There was no way that rope would break.

Kullins deliberately twisted until his eyes met Derek's, and he took a moment of vast, vile pleasure at Derek's helpless devastation.

Derek's mind was a mess of manic thoughts and helpless struggles. Hectic and fleeting thoughts of important moments in his life flashed before his eyes.

He was engaged once. To a woman who betrayed him; who saw his pursuit against the paranormal as a joke.

He had taken on a prodigy who fell to hell, and a prodigy who stood against him.

He taught students in a lecture theatre. University students willing to entertain the notion of demons and ghosts.

This was all for other people.

He never did anything that could help himself.

So this is what it's like to die...

Thoughts swirled around his head like locusts, his insecurities highlighting that he had done everything wrong. His final thoughts acting as a final attack of furious anxieties, telling him that redemption was something he would not be afforded.

The executioner descended the steps. His eyes peered through his mask, looking upon Derek's.

They weren't the eyes of a killer. They were the eyes of a man who was too afraid not to kill. A man petrified that he would be next, should he not carry out his orders.

Those were the eyes of weakness.

Derek attempted to drag himself away, to pull himself along the bumpy ground. The bumps of the cement ripped his trousers and cut his knees, leaving a trail of red across the damp surface.

The worst part of it all was that Derek knew these few yards he gained would do nothing. That thought was imprinted pertinently against the front of his mind, high-lighting his pathetically helpless state.

But he couldn't do nothing. He had to try, however feeble an attempt it may be.

He could have minutes left.

It depended on how merciful the governor would be.

Would he be asked to give his final words?

What would his final words be?

In abandoned desperation, he tried to think of something wise, something that would say "screw you" to the whole estab-lishment.

But he came up with nothing. He knew that if he gave himself another hour, he would. It was something the French called l'esprit de l'escalier, literally translated as 'the wit of the staircase.' It was a phrase for those moments when you thought of something to say after the retort was relevant.

Such pathetic, unhelpful thoughts were appearing to him in a time of grave need.

What good was his useless knowledge to him now?

He could recite every exorcism prayer, conduct a successful séance, or banish an unclean spirit from your home.

But he could not save himself from being dragged across a prison courtyard to his death.

The executioner's hefty boots stood firmly before him, halting his useless attempt to escape.

Derek rolled onto his back and peered up at the cowardly eyes staring down at him.

"You don't want to do this, do you?" he asked.

The executioner's eyes narrowed into a glare.

"You don't have to. You know it's wrong. You know you can say no."

The executioner bent over Derek and took the scruff of his collar in a small, scrawny fist.

"You'll shut the hell up if you know what's good for you," came the voice of a little man trying his best to sound tough.

Derek had no choice but to allow himself to be dragged helplessly across the courtyard, toward the gallows, watching his fate grow ever closer.

38

This was more than Oscar had ever been prepared for.

But he wasn't just fighting for himself anymore.

Or Derek.

Or even Julian.

He remembered what April had said.

This thing was attacking both Julian and Derek. They needed to be rid of it at the prison, and at Julian's home. The entity needed to be defeated on all fronts.

Only, this meant the logical conclusion was that if Oscar couldn't defeat it…

Then April couldn't either.

Meaning that she would perish too.

She was relying on him.

He let those words sink in.

She is relying. On me.

For a fleeting moment, Oscar missed when his life was as simple as working at Morrison's, then going home, touching himself, and playing on the Xbox until he fell asleep.

That was the old Oscar. He was gone now.

It was time to be solid. To be confident. To be fierce.

No more forgetting silly incantations.

No more wussing out every time he went to tell April how he felt.

No more allowing Julian to speak to him like a petulant child.

It was time to stand strong. Stand sturdy. Stand tall.

Time to be firmly defiant in the face of evil.

Or something along those lines...

Oscar withdrew the crucifix from his pocket. He pointed it authoritatively toward the prison entrance. The entry point looked vacant, but something with the power to take him clean off his feet and into the air was strong, visible or not.

"Back off, unclean spirit!" Oscar screamed, feeling a tinge of embarrassment as his voice broke. He pushed any feelings of embarrassment to the back of his mind and persevered forward. "I demand you allow me passage into this prison!"

He edged closer and closer, holding his cross firmly, staring intently at the prison doors.

As he approached the door he felt a strong surge of wind fight against him, but he wrapped his unyielding fingers around his cross and stood strong.

"I come to you today, bowing in my heart, asking for protection from the evil one!" Oscar shouted at the malevolent force battering against him. He could feel his hair waving against frequent surges of wind, but he was not deterred. He pushed against the gust with all his might. "We are assailed moment by moment with evil images that leave us vulnerable to every sin of every kind. Against this sin, I beg your salvation!"

The force pushed harder still against Oscar as he approached the threshold, but Oscar forced his heavy legs forward, his cross before him, bellowing his prayers against the wind.

He skidded backwards but refuted the force, treading with all his might.

"Surround me!" he continued, raising his voice higher. "Surround me! Encompass me with Your strength and Your might! Let all that take refuge be glad, let them ever sing for joy! Let my voice sing for joy, let your love be ever present, surround me with your good graces – surround me!"

His foot stepped over the threshold. The door went to slam against him, but he held out his cross and remained strong.

"Surround me!"

As if he was being afforded an extra layer of protection, the door stuck mid-swipe. It flapped back and forth, the evil from within fighting against the good forces from outside, and it was no one's guess who was going to win.

Oscar strode further forward, trying to force his way in, pushing against the resistance.

"You may shelter us, Your name may exult you, for it is You that blesses the righteous man, and call me righteous as I fight in Your name, O Lord!"

Another step.

He managed another step.

The door wafted, beating against itself with fever and ferocity.

"Surround me with your favour – surround me with your shield! Allow me safe passage to this house of evil!"

With a surge of strength, Oscar forced himself into the prison, diving upon the floor.

The door slammed behind him.

Oscar remained on his knees in the middle of a corridor, feeling the wind rushing around him in a vigorous tornado, an aggressive swirling of evil gusts encompassing him in a malicious, powerful force.

Screams echoed along the corridor and assaulted his ears.

Wails of pain and torture blasted against him.

Cries of the suffering, begs of the tormented, racing across the echoes of the chaotic wind until it became deafening.

Oscar covered his ears, unable to take the battering of his eardrums. It was louder than any music concert he had ever been to; it was as if loudspeakers were pinned against his head, forcing manic vibrations to pound through his ears and fill his mind with disorder.

He couldn't let it beat him.

He couldn't.

He had to continue.

"Strengthen us in the power of Your might!" he shouted, unable to hear his own voice above the noise. "Dress us in Your armour, fill my blood and bones, against the spiritual forces of wickedness and evil!"

The screams bellowed louder still.

Everyone who had ever suffered, died, been tortured, disembowelled, hurt, left to go crazy; all of them reached inside Oscar's head and pulverised his cranium. His head throbbed with the power of a hundred shrieks, trying to make him crazy, trying to take his sanity from him in one desperate act of servitude.

"Surround me!" he persisted, his voice fading in the ear-splitting racket. His ears were pounding, hurting, burning as if they were about to burst.

"You are our keeper! And I beg you – surround me with your protection!"

Screaming. Crying. Twisting his mind.

"Surround me!"

Forcing his head into a manic haze of thrashing suffering.

"Surround me!"

Suddenly, it stopped.

The wind. The voices. The noise.

Silence.

Assuming it was a trick, he did not move. He kept his hands

over his ears, kept his crouched knees still. His heart beat against his chest, his hands pushing against his ears.

He opened an eyelid.

Then the other.

He peered around himself.

He waited, as if expecting something to pounce at him.

Nothing did.

He removed his hands.

The walls crumbled. The bars at the end of the corridor were rusted. The floor he knelt upon ripped his jeans with bumps and broken fragments.

But there was silence.

Nothing fought against him.

It had worked.

He was in.

THOUGHTS OF DOUBT AND FEAR FORCED APRIL TO CONTEMPLATE her decision.

Had she done the right thing?

She had basically just left Oscar to deal with an incredibly powerful, furious malevolent force.

I'm an idiot. What have I done?

He was talented, yes – but inexperienced.

But so was she once. She had to be left to make her own mistakes and learn from them. Only after that did she seize her talent and become the force she had become.

But she'd left him there.

On his own. Helpless.

I had no choice.

They didn't have Derek or Julian, which was going to make this so much tougher. And, what's more, the spirit that was battling against them was clearly battling at both the prison and Julian's home. If she had stayed with him and defeated the prison's entity, it would have just reformed. Both sides of this thing needed to be destroyed.

So she had gotten in her car and sped away, regretfully

watching him grow smaller in her rear-view mirror. Watching as he stood, readying himself, then disappearing from view.

If only she could know how he was doing.

No.

Stop it.

This is no time for reservations.

She had faith in him.

With all that she had seen, she had come to believe in the impossible.

It was time to stand tall, stand strong, and above all else, focus.

She wasn't going to have it any easier at her end.

She brought the car to a stop against the side of the road, ignoring the double yellow lines. She didn't have time to find an appropriate parking space and, being honest, she didn't give a damn whether they chose to give her a ticket at that particular moment.

She rushed out of the car and sprinted up the path to Julian's flat.

"Julian!" she shouted, banging her fists against the door. "Julian, open up!"

There was no response, but there was definite noise.

A frantic clatter, followed by a shattering smash.

The door rattled, battling against its hinges, the wickedness within berating her, fuelling her fear.

She put her ear closer to the door and listened.

The sound of objects clattering against walls, furniture smashing, accompanied by hysterical shouting.

Multiple voices of hysterical shouting.

None of them Julian's.

She tried the door handle, on the off-chance that, maybe, it was unlocked – but she had no such luck.

She stood back, took a few paces run-up, and launched her shoulder into the door.

It did nothing. It barely even shook. It hurt her shoulder more than it hurt the door.

What next?

She ran to the kitchen window and tried to peer inside. Flickers of shadows bounced around, but she was at too much of an angle to see the main commotion.

I could smash the glass...

But what with?

Then it hit her.

The spare key. She had a spare key.

But where was it? She didn't have time to go home and get it – she had no assurances that Julian was still alive, and the chances were decreasing by the minute.

Then she realised.

"You idiot," she muttered to herself as she turned back to her car, where she kept the spare key in the glove compartment.

A traffic warden was already writing out a ticket.

They don't waste a moment, do they...

"Did you know you're on double yellow lines?"

"Couldn't care less, mate."

She opened the car, reached inside the glove compartment, grabbed the key, and sprinted back toward the flat.

She went to shove the key in but, with her desperation to get inside and with the struggle to fit it in the trembling lock, she fumbled it and dropped it on the floor.

"Crap!"

She picked it up, willed herself to concentrate, and placed it into the lock. She had to be of sound mind if she was going to do anything, and she was already letting this thing get the better of her.

She opened the door and stepped inside.

The room was a crazed chaos. A tornado of broken objects

battered the walls, spinning in a ferocious circle so quick and so violent that April could not get anywhere near it.

She edged forward, holding a hand out, guiding her way through the anarchy that masked her vision.

Through the pandemonium, she saw him.

Julian.

In the centre of the violently spinning broken glass and his destroyed possessions.

Lying on the floor amongst a mess of ripped paper, his eyes closed.

He wore nothing but pyjama trousers, which were rags, ripped and torn to shreds. His torso was covered in cuts and bruises, and numerous marks decorated the flaking skin of his pale face.

Most of the cuts engrained upon his body were in the shape of an upside-down crucifix. A symbol that represented Satanism – as a mocking of the Holy Trinity, and a representation of the unholy trinity; removing the Father, the Son and the Holy Spirit, and replacing them with the devil, the antichrist, and the false prophet.

If such marks were being cut into his body, then it was a sure, unequivocal sign that something deadly and of pure evil was at work here, and they were in grave danger.

"Julian!" April screamed.

In an immediate response, she was launched off her feet and thrown out of the flat, forced to land harshly on her back. As she groaned with pain, the front door slammed shut.

40

THE CORRIDORS OF THE PRISON SEEMED TO HAVE GROWN INTO A vast maze. They were no longer the clean, sterile corridors Oscar had previously walked down – they were now mossy, rusting, broken-down corridors of a building that had been left uncared for.

And they seemed to lead to nowhere.

The route had turned into a perplexing labyrinth, entwining like weeds around a tree, growing obscurely in each direction.

Oscar was in severe danger of getting lost.

He searched for a sign, searched for something that would indicate where he needed to go.

Finally, he found it. A sign that read *A Wing*.

That was Derek's wing, he was sure of it – he recalled discovering that Derek was in the 'haunted' cell, which was A Wing Cell 25.

He followed the sign, stepping carefully and cautiously through the darkness. Night had fully descended upon the prison and there were no lamps to guide Oscar's way.

He took out his iPhone, selected the flashlight option and

directed it forward, peering into the distance just to find a vague nothingness. Darkness led him further into the endless corridor but, with no other indication of where to go other than the signage, he kept his hand against the wall to help him guide his way, and slowly stepped forward.

His faint footsteps echoed lightly against the stony floor. His hand ran over the cracks and bumps of the walls, giving him a small amount of reassurance that he was safe.

Safe.

"Hah."

He couldn't help but grunt at the ridiculousness of the concept. Safety was an illusion that had been painted for him by naiveté. Just a year ago he would have thought he was safe; now he knew better. True safety never really wraps its comforting arms around you – there is always something lurking, ready to rip it away.

And such a statement was truer now more than ever.

He realised he was shivering. The prison grew colder the further he made it in. He knew enough to know that this was a sure sign that the evil dwelling within these halls was growing stronger.

But that wasn't the real reason he was shaking.

His lunch turned over in the pit of his stomach and he did all he could to not bring it up. He was terrified. This thing had managed to launch him off his feet before he even made it into the prison. Now, he was nearing the dead centre, and he knew it was just a matter of time until he came to a face-to-face confrontation.

With a spark of luck, he found himself next to the door with a big, clear sign upon it: *A Wing*.

He put his hand against the door to open it.

Paused.

This was too easy.

Luck would not be on his side. This thing had taken over a whole prison; it was too powerful.

He had found A Wing through reordered corridors that appeared to be leading nowhere. It just didn't make sense.

Was it a trick?

The corridors had twisted and contorted, changed and messed up his path. The prison could have kept him searching for days, kept him trapped and lost in the depths of the hell-hole permanently if it wished.

So why had the prison allowed him to find this wing?

What were its intentions?

With an extra level of caution, he pushed the door open, elongating its squeak as he opened it slowly.

He edged in, pointing his light into the wing, moving it from left to right, up and down, inspecting every crevasse and every corner.

The wing appeared as he expected. Rusting cell doors, mould on the walls, and a strong smell of damp. It was an ageing, decrepit, pit of decay that looked as if it had been uninhabited for years.

As he made it into the wing, he rotated in full circles, aware that something could jump out onto his back at any moment. He shone his light all around, listening to every sound, inspecting every wall, every floor, and the bars to every cell.

A smell of rotting meat hit him in the face, forcing him to choke. It was overwhelming. A repugnant smell pushing against him.

It could only mean one thing.

It was the indication that something was in there with him.

"Hello?" Oscar offered, his voice reverberating.

He edged forward, and the smell just continued getting stronger.

"I know you're there," Oscar spoke, more confidently than he felt. "Show yourself."

He turned around once more, shining his light across every wall and into every cell. There were so many cells; three floors of them. Something could easily be waiting, ready to pounce.

"I'm not scared of you," he lied. "You may as well come out and face me."

Clap. Clap. Clap.

Oscar froze. His breath caught in his throat.

He daren't move.

Clap. Clap. Clap.

He shone the light into every cell, to the ceiling, behind him, before him.

Clap. Clap. Clap.

"You don't scare me. Show yourself."

The clapping grew louder.

Clap. Clap. Clap.

It came from a cell to the right.

Oscar immediately turned his light to the nearest cell and watched with astonishment as a figure emerged, lit only by the light from his phone. As the silhouette came into the vague luminescence, Oscar scrutinised its appearance. It was a man, wearing a prison officer's uniform; the same uniform as the man who had led them into the prison on his first visit.

The man continued to clap sarcastically, a large grin beneath his moustache, his greying hair swept to one side.

Oscar's light flickered against the cell number the man had just walked out of.

Cell 25.

"Who are you?" Oscar demanded, rooted to the spot.

The man halted a few yards away from Oscar, ceasing his clapping, and giving a mocking bow.

"Well done, my boy," the man spoke. "Well done."

"Who are you?"

"I am a prison officer. And I believe you are... Oscar? Is that right? One of *his* friends?"

"You are not a prison officer here. This prison hasn't been used in four years."

"Okay, I will correct myself, my dear fellow – I *used* to be a prison officer here. Now I am dead."

Oscar kept his light shining on this man's face, staring at him intently, mentally preparing himself for any sudden move.

This was too easy. Too simple.

The entity had directed him to Derek's cell and had just revealed itself. Entered polite conversation, instead of furiously attacking Oscar with everything it had.

It didn't make any sense.

"Where's Derek?" Oscar commanded.

"Derek? Remind me..."

"Give it a rest, I know you have him. Where is he? Is he in Cell 25?"

The prison officer's grin extended, growing into a vicious smirk.

"Answer me this, my boy. What do you plan to do should you find him?"

Oscar didn't respond. He didn't want to bite. He knew what it wanted.

"A young lad like you. Do you *really* think you could save him?"

Why did it matter?

Why did the entity care about whether or not he thought he could save Derek?

Why was it just talking to him, making idle conversation?

"He is safe with us now. Part of the prison. Where he will stay."

Then he realised.

This was all for show.

It was a distraction. Keeping Oscar occupied.

The entity didn't care about him, it was Derek it was after –

and this apparition was just doing its best to keep Oscar away from whatever they were doing.

"What have you done with him?"

Oscar ran past the entity, into Cell 25.

The prison officer instantly manifested itself into a large demonic creature, ravenous fangs exuding from its bloody jaw.

Oscar held out his cross and sprinted past, finding himself alone in what used to be Derek's home.

It was empty.

Oscar ran to the cell window and looked out upon the courtyard.

That's when he saw Derek.

Being led up a set of stairs to the gallows, where an empty noose awaited him.

41

APRIL LEAPT DEFIANTLY TO HER FEET, HER FISTS CLENCHED, blood firing through her veins. She had battled enough evil things in her time to know the typical tactics of intimidation. This didn't scare her.

She charged at the door, leading with her shoulder, putting all her weight behind it, and barged open the door, falling to her feet amongst the mess of Julian's ill-kept living room.

"Julian!" she yelped, having to squint to be able to see him inside the hysterically gushing wind, isolated by thrashing objects that created a circular force around him.

She needed to get in there with him, inside of the spinning anarchy. That way she could get through to him, beseech him, help him battle from the inside.

She dragged herself to her feet, resisting the force that attempted to repel her, refusing to be pushed back down. She put all her weight behind her, pressing her feet down against the stained, cracked floor, forcing herself forward.

It was like wading through water. She did all she could to resist the entity's force, relying solely on will and determination.

She reached out toward the objects circling Julian, reaching her hand toward the revolving mayhem, until she just about poked a hand inside the edge of the spinning force.

"Ow!"

She instinctively withdrew her hand.

Something had cut her. A slit along her palm throbbed with pain, blood seeping down her wrist.

Broken pieces of furniture, splinters, sharp objects, kitchen knives, ripped paper – everything that had been in that flat was part of that forcefield separating her from Julian. What had cut her could have been anything.

Luckily, she had slowly edged her hand in. She knew that if she'd tried jumping through, she would have more than an injured palm.

She held her wrist for a few moments, staring intently at her gushing open wound, her incoherent thoughts racing to produce a way that she could stop the bleeding.

There was nothing she could use. She was going to have to endure it.

Julian was the priority.

She looked around, searching for some way to get to him.

"Julian!" she tried again. "Julian, wake up!"

It was no good.

His body remained still, entwined with the disorder of the room. Ravaged by whatever was tormenting him.

"Julian, please!"

She was sure she could hear a chuckle echo throughout the room, mocking her helplessness.

She sighed.

She needed to think of something.

Maybe if I could create some kind of shield...

She turned back to the room, searching it, looking for anything that could help her.

Some of the remains of Julian's desk rested against the far

wall, nudging ever so slightly back and forth on the outskirts of the wind. She seized a plank and placed it cautiously into the mess surging through the air.

She withdrew it, looking upon its resulting state – a piece of shaved and shattered mess.

"Shit!"

She took a deep inward breath and let it out. Stayed calm. Told herself not to panic. Told herself to ride out this storm.

"Julian, wake up, it's me!" she tried once more, fearing that the only way to get to him would be to appeal to his strength, and hope that he heard her through the howling gale. It was his guilt that was controlling this, that was fuelling this – that negative energy was powering this entity.

"Julian, come on!"

He stirred, groaned, but only to shift in his unconscious state.

"Damn it, Julian, you listen to me now!"

His nose twitched. His hands flexed.

"Julian, I know you can hear me!"

His eyelids fluttered.

She knew he could hear her.

But she needed a break. A momentary weakness in the spirit that could allow her to jump through the mess, to get closer to him so he could hear her loud and clear.

But how?

She couldn't create a shield. She couldn't protect herself from it. There was nothing she could do.

Then she thought – maybe she didn't have to.

Oscar could create that weakness.

Any success he had at the prison would surely impact on the strength of the entity this end.

She had to continue to have faith.

Once again, she was reliant on the two men in her life.

42

THE DEMONIC APPARITION HOVERED IN THE DOORWAY TO THE cell, its deformed mouth now distorted into an even larger grin. Horns twisted from its head, blood dribbled from its chin, and a sharp tail thrashed against the walls of the cell.

Oscar shook his head.

He could not be afraid.

He could not let himself be deterred through even the slightest tinge of dread.

This thing was powering itself on fear. Oscar could not give it that.

"You're going to kill him?" Oscar asked defiantly. "And for what?"

"This man has tormented Hell for decades," a large, booming voice bashed against the cell walls. "This will be our final revenge."

"I won't let you take him."

"There is nothing you can do about it."

Oscar held out his cross and charged forward. As long as he had this crucifix in his hand, he knew that he–

The demon's snapping red tail cracked the cross out of

Oscar's hands so quickly he barely noticed, sending it soaring to the far wall, smashing into pieces.

Oscar's eyes looked to this creature, feigning defiance, his heart thudding against his chest.

"Cover my mind with the helmet of Your salvation," Oscar spoke the prayer, unable to force the shaking out of his voice. "Surround me constantly, as I am Your child. Fix my thoughts with–"

Oscar rose into the air by his chest, continuing to rise, the rest of his body hanging loosely like a rag doll.

He felt his arms fixing in place, growing rigidly behind his back. An invisible force was constraining him, holding him still, pulling him tighter.

"Keep the enemy at bay," he persevered, his voice coming out as a dim croak. "Calm my emotions with the peace of Your presence. Help me follow Your command and–"

Something constricted tightly around his neck. He could feel thick fingers around his throat, tightening. Long fingers, with sharp claws, wrapping themselves around his oesophagus. He tried to speak, but it was too tight, and barely a whimper could escape his lips.

He couldn't speak his prayer.

That was my only chance.

He struggled for breath. He thrashed for it, but his body was held so firmly in place not a single muscle could move.

He was suffocating.

I'm going to die.

His eyes remained wide open, staring with terror at the face of the true form of this thing glaring back at him, searing into his eyes. Enjoying his helpless asphyxiation. Enjoying the look of terror as an acknowledgement that this could be the end spread across his fearful face.

It was big. It was vile. And its demonic features were petrifying.

Its cackles turned to hysterics.

"You fool!" its voice echoed with a dirty gust of wind against Oscar's face. "You really thought you stood a chance…"

Blots of light obscured his vision.

He could feel his body going. Life draining.

Soon he would be unconscious.

Then he would die.

Without ever telling April how he felt. Without ever proving Julian wrong. Without ever meaning a damn thing to this world.

Something brushed against his hand.

Something else, like a gentle breeze, enclosing it, holding it. It was small, like a child's hand.

There was something else in there with them.

The entity's triumphant grin turned to an aggressive snarl, glaring at something behind Oscar's back.

"Let – him – go!" cried a young girl's voice, a girl who couldn't be more than a child.

He felt the grip around his throat loosen, and he managed to gasp a gulp of air. He breathed whilst he still could, taking in all the oxygen he was able.

The firm hold on his body loosened. He was still held in place, but he could wiggle his toes and flex his arms.

"Leave him be!" the young girl's voice repeated.

The entity growled.

Oscar dropped to the floor, landing heavily on his elbow. He grabbed it, at first willing the pain away, then feeling grateful that the only pain he felt was a sore elbow.

"You will not take him!" the entity bellowed, then disappeared into the air.

Oscar rolled onto his back, searching for whatever it was that had appeared behind him.

It was a young girl, dressed in clothing from a long time ago. From at least five centuries in the past.

213

"Who are you?" Oscar gasped.

"My name is Elizabeth," the spirit told him. "Derek's in danger. I tried to warn him. You need to save your friend."

"I need to get to the courtyard. How can I do this?"

"I will grant you safe passage, but you need to go now."

He clambered to his feet, nodding gratefully at the girl.

"Thank you."

"Go!"

He turned, stumbling to his feet, sprinting as fast as he could out of the cell and through the wing.

Numerous faces screamed at him as he passed them, claws swiping, jaws snapping. Trying to grab him. Trying to swipe him away.

But none of them reached him, thanks to Elizabeth.

The entity had been momentarily weakened, if only for a few fleeting seconds.

Within minutes he had reached the edge of the courtyard, and Derek was in sight.

But Derek could not see Oscar.

Because Derek had a bag over his head, a noose around his neck, and the executioner was just about to push him off the steps.

43

The twirling objects around Julian slowed down.

Yes!

Oscar had done something.

But she knew it wouldn't last long.

Jumping over that barrier was a risk. It could start again any second. It could still hurt her.

But she had no time to second guess herself.

She had to take the opportunity, and do it hastily.

She closed her eyes, pressing her eyelids together as firmly as she could, and took a large leap forward.

She opened her eyes.

Julian lay below her.

The chaotic mess resumed its manic spinning, encasing both her and Julian within it.

"Julian," she pleaded, shaking him. "Come on."

He groaned. But it was something.

"Julian!"

He began to stir, his eyes flickering open, closed, open, closed.

"Julian, wake up, it's me!"

His eyes hazily opened, peering upwards, squinting at April, his vision attempting to refocus.

"Thank God, Julian. It's me!"

"...April?" he asked feebly, his eyes closing once again.

She shook him.

"No, do not go back to sleep!"

His eyes opened.

"Listen to me, Julian, you are under attack!"

"What?" he mumbled. "Where is Anna?"

"Anna is *dead*, Julian; she has been for years. And it's *not* your fault."

Julian groggily rotated his head, peering at his surroundings, watching their prison spin around them.

The room fell silent. Everything still spun, but as if going into slow motion. April watched Julian, hoping he would come back, praying for him to return.

"Julian, you need to destroy this."

"Destroy what?"

"It's your guilt that's doing this. You're a wreck. It's some kind of entity and it is feeding off you. You and Derek. You need to stop feeding it."

He groaned and turned onto his side, closing his eyes.

"Go away, April, and leave me alone."

"No!" she refuted, and shook him more aggressively.

He turned to her with a scowl.

"What the fuck are you doing?"

"Saving your life!" she shouted, her eyes filling with tears, her face breaking, her heart beating. "You took me off the streets, remember? You taught me how to harness my powers. You did that!"

"I know who you are..." He tried to turn back over again.

"Then stop looking away from me, you arsehole!"

He turned his face back to her, his eyes widening, growing angry.

Emotions overcame her. Every piece of her cried for him, longed for him to understand, to return to her. For years and years, she had been under his wing, and now he was falling into the dark abyss and she could not take it.

"Who the hell do you think—"

"You did *not* kill Anna! Nor did Derek. You both did all you could for her, it just was *not* enough. You *need* to understand that right now."

"You don't know anything about it."

"I know that your shitty reaction is shitty enough to create this mess. You need to be strong, Julian. You need to be strong, or we're all dead. Me, you, Oscar, Derek – we are all goners."

Julian's eyes met hers. For the first time, she saw his vulnerability. His weakness. He looked back at her, full of dismay, full of pain.

"You don't understand…" he whispered.

"Yes, I do."

"I watched her die…"

"And she would have died sooner, and far more violently, if you two hadn't stepped in!"

Tears trickled down his cheeks.

This was good.

He was facing it.

He was finally facing his demons.

"You need to be strong!"

"I can't, April. I can't keep being the strong one, the one who can never do any wrong, that's not who I am…"

"I'm not asking you to be who you are not. I'm just asking you to be…"

"To be what?"

Her eyes broke.

"To be the man who took me off the streets and gave me a home," she beseeched him, peering sincerely into his blood-shot, fading eyes, her cheeks soaked with tears. "The man who taught me how to harness my power. The man who saved me from the gutter."

"April…"

"To be the man who taught me my greatest lesson."

"Which is?"

She grabbed the back of his sweaty hair, turning his face toward hers, forcing him to look in her eyes, forcing him to see the pain she was having to endure.

"That the biggest obstacle you will ever have to overcome is yourself."

He watched her intently.

Watched as Derek's wise words escaped her lips.

Watched as those words washed over him, cleansing him with a clear mind.

She was right.

"Help me to my feet," he told her.

She helped him gain balance, helping him to stand upright and assuredly before the sickening state his flat had been left in.

No more.

"*Leave!*" he bellowed. "Leave my flat, you bastard of hell!"

Screeches entwined with screams, and shouts filled the air, accompanied by an ominous grey smoke.

"You don't scare me," he boldly revealed, narrowing his eyes.

The force grew weaker. Objects flew into the wall, out of the entwining circle. Glasses exploded. Heavier pieces of furniture fell upon the floor, the entity no longer with the strength to be able to hold them afloat.

"Go back to Hell where you belong."

The noise grew less.

The chaos dullened.

April had done her part.

It was up to Oscar now.

44

Oscar launched himself forward, sprinting across the courtyard as fast as his aching legs would take him.

Prison officers stood vacantly, watching with absent eyes. As he ran amongst them, each of them turned and transformed into a transparent apparition, launching themselves toward Oscar.

Oscar raised his arms and shielded his face, saving himself from the surge of wind that each demonic force thrust against him.

Each one unsteadied his balance, pushing against him, forcing him to stumble.

But he would not be discouraged.

The executioner saw Oscar coming and decided it was time.

With a forceful kick, the man pushed Derek off the steps.

Derek, with a bag over his head and a noose tied tightly around his neck, dangled helplessly. He tried kicking, but his legs – his legs weren't what they used to be. The dreaded sound of him choking carried across the courtyard. It was all that could be heard.

Oscar decided it was time to stop shielding himself.

He stood tall, his arms to his side, his fists clenched, his face a snarling visage of determination.

He strode forward. Another prison officer launched a demonic attack at him, but he screamed in its face, refuting its power, sending it away.

Derek didn't have long.

Minutes.

Oscar couldn't waste a moment.

He charged forward, the gallows growing closer.

A man stepped in front of him. A man who towered over him with a sadistic glare. His unsettling presence alone sent waves of malicious sin charging in every direction like volts of electricity.

He terrified Oscar. Out of everything he had faced so far, this was what mortified him.

Oscar knew who this man was.

This was Kullins.

This was the prison governor.

"Get out of my way," Oscar instructed, not faltering in his confident strides forward.

The governor's mouth opened and extended. In an aggressive gust of wind, Oscar was sent onto his back.

He stood back up straight away, refusing to be pushed down.

"You'll need to do better than that!" he claimed.

The governor smirked, a glint in his eye, as if to say, "Challenge accepted." He transformed, and he was the governor no more.

His arms extended into large claws, his teeth manifesting into vile fangs dripping with blood, his eyes turning a mixture of dark yellow and red.

Oscar felt goose bumps prick. His heart thudding. He fell to his back beneath the snarling, ravenous creature that presented itself before him. It was like the fierce beast he had faced on A

Wing, but bigger, bloodier, and full of infinite evil. A demon of the underworld, looming over the courtyard, sinful eyes and piercing claws that elongated into large, sharp points.

"Okay, you did better..." Oscar conceded.

He glanced at Derek.

His body was thrashing.

He was still alive. But not for long.

The prayers he had been using so far wouldn't be good enough. He knew what he'd have to use.

The incantation.

The one he had previously forgotten.

As soon as he realised which prayer he would have to use his anxiety took over, and every word he knew slipped out of his mind like water through fingers.

The demon's claw struck against the ground. Oscar rolled to his side, narrowly missing the strike, but the force of its fist shook the ground enough to make Oscar rise into the air then collapse against the bumpy gravel.

"Shit, come on!" he willed himself.

He closed his eyes.

Calmed his mind.

He could feel the demon's claw swipe through the air toward him.

He thought back to that book he had reread again and again, desperate not to make the same mistake.

He had it.

God damn, I have it!

"I know my transgressions," he began, "and my sin is ever before me."

He opened his eyes.

The demon's claw halted above him.

"Against you, you alone, I have sinned," Oscar continued, rising to his feet. "Indeed, I was born guilty, but I hide my face from your sins, and blot out all my iniquities."

The demon growled, a force of dirty wind spewing in Oscar's direction.

But Oscar knew it was a feeble attempt at intimidating him. The demon recognised the prayer, and knew it had nowhere to go.

"Create in me a clean heart, oh God, and put a new and right spirit within this place."

He stepped forward, edging toward the beast, his eyes focussed intently on his deadliest enemy.

Out of the corner of his eyes, he could see Derek's body struggling less. A state of unconsciousness descended upon him.

"In the name, power and authority of Jesus Christ, Lord and Saviour God, Holy Ghost, do the work I need right now, as I make these proclamations."

The demon howled in agony, curling up into a helpless ball upon the floor.

The executioner that stood beside the gallows looked to Oscar with terrified eyes, transformed into a puff of air, and disappeared into the night sky.

"I renounce and reject sins, and I–"

Shit.

He froze.

This is where I messed up before.

He looked upon the demon.

"I renounce and reject sins, and I–"

The demon ceased its writhing and looked back at Oscar.

"I renounce and reject sins, and I…"

The demon grinned.

As did Oscar.

"I renounce and reject sins – *and any sinful items kept here!*"

Fooled you.

The demon howled in a final shriek of anguish, its skin tingeing, smoke rising from its body.

"Be gone, beast! Be banished from the place you once resided! *Be gone!*"

The demon burst into a ball of flames, and with one final, high-pitched screech, plunged downwards into the ground, sailing back to hell where it belonged.

Oscar rushed up the stairs and dove onto the top of the gallows. He swung it with all his force, coercing the wooden beams to unbalance, swinging and swinging until, eventually, the contraption collapsed onto the floor and broke into a few shards of wood.

Oscar leapt to Derek's side, removed the bag, and untied the noose.

Derek's eyes were closed.

Oscar rested his ear against Derek's chest, listening for breath, listening for a heartbeat.

At first, nothing.

Then, there it was.

A faint boom. Slow and soft, but there nonetheless.

Derek's chest rose up and down, slowly, weakly.

Derek's eyes opened.

But he wasn't all there. He was groggy, behind the eyes somewhere, his mind a hazy mess.

But he was alive.

I did it.

He helped Derek to his feet and dragged him back to the car park.

He felt silly phoning for a taxi after all that happened, but it arrived within half an hour, and the driver helped carry Derek into the backseat.

"What the hell have you been doing 'ere?" the taxi driver inquired. "This ain't been open for years."

"You know," Oscar replied as they drove away from the prison and toward Julian's flat, "you've told me that just a tad too late."

223

45

OSCAR WAS OUT OF THE TAXI LIKE A BULLET, RUNNING TOWARD Julian's flat with everything he had.

The taxi driver helped Derek out of the car, tutting at Oscar's lack of empathy. Oscar didn't care.

He had to check on April.

The door was open.

Oscar ran through it and came to a skidding halt.

The room was a huge mess. Broken objects lay across the floor with such frequency he had to walk precariously onto each of the sparse gaps on the floor, trying not to step on anything sharp.

Julian sat beside April on the sofa, with a warm blanket around him.

As soon as Oscar entered the room, April stood.

They stared.

April smiled, walking toward Oscar, tiptoeing through the mess of the floor until she finally reached him.

Derek entered behind them and made his way to the sofa beside Julian, but Oscar only cared about one thing.

April smiled. Oscar smiled back. Their arms flung around each other in a warm, tight, loving embrace.

"You clever, clever boy," she told him. "You are so clever. I'm so proud of you!"

"Well..."

"Really!" She pulled back and looked him in the eyes, keeping her arms firmly and gratefully around him. "You did amazingly. You took on the entire place by yourself. I just..."

Her smile said it all.

"I know," he answered, pretending to be modest, but was already blushing from all the delightful praise she was endowing on him. "It was tough, but I got there in the end."

With a surge of confidence, he held her tight.

He was going to say it.

How he felt.

Everything he had kept inside.

"April, listen, I have something to tell you. I feel–"

"Oh, shut up!"

She pulled his face toward hers and planted a soft, delicate, earth-shattering kiss upon his lips. The whole room spun, his whole body tingling, every piece of him filling with innocent joy.

He closed his eyes and sank into it, allowing the kiss to get more and more passionate, tying his arms around her, pulling her in close. He could feel her body against him, he could feel her breasts pressing against his chest, could feel her soft, warm lips pressing firmly against his. Butterflies swarmed around his chest, fluttering free at last.

Eventually, their lips parted, and they stood in an embrace with their foreheads rested against each other, gazing happily into each other's eyes.

"Wow," was all he could say.

"I know."

She smiled back with that sweet smile that made his legs go weak.

"You could have just done this to begin with," he playfully told her.

"I know, but then I'd have missed out on watching you squirm, you idiot."

"You mean, you knew all along?"

"Of course I bloody knew!"

She chuckled as she pulled him in closer once more, pushing her lips against his, holding him close. All their emotions, their stress, their longing, everything came out in that kiss.

It was Oscar's favourite moment of his life so far, and one he wished never ended.

THREE WEEKS LATER

46

Jason sat at his desk, pictures of the case strewn across the table.

A weak knock tapped against his door. Jason was taken aback to see Julian cautiously hovering. He looked far better than he had when Jason last saw him. His hair was well-groomed, he was dressed tidily, and the vile odour was no longer following him around.

"Julian?" Jason asked apprehensively.

"I've come to apologise," Julian announced. "You saw me in a pretty bad state. Stuff was happening. That wasn't me."

Jason leant back in his seat.

"Really?"

"Yes, really. But I'm fine now. Really, I am. You said you had a case for me?"

Jason chewed on the end of his pen.

Could he really still trust Julian? After the state he'd seen him in?

"I did."

"You did?"

"The case has gotten far, far worse. At first, it was just a deceased doctor. Now it's..."

"What?" Julian asked, stepping forward, taking the seat opposite Jason. "What is it?"

"Now it's the entire children's ward of the hospital. Something is happening to them. Something no one can explain."

Julian smiled. He was glad to be back to work.

"Tell me about it, I want to help," he told Jason assuredly.

* * *

Derek shuffled the newspaper, rereading the headline, still in disbelief.

Man Found Guilty of Murder Gone Missing on Route to Prison

"Remarkable," he whispered. He checked the date. 29th October 2013.

Four years ago.

"I don't suppose you knew about this?" Derek asked, feeling foolish for asking such an obvious question.

"I found it in the library archives," Julian answered. "Took me four hours to find – it was pretty well hidden. It says two officers and a transported inmate completely disappeared from the vehicle in transit. They don't give a name. I imagine that's thanks to our friends in Rome."

Derek folded the newspaper up. "Curious."

"Of course, I never gave much thought to it at the time. I can't even remember seeing the story reported. And I would never given thought to it, considering I visited you shortly after in Gloucester prison." Julian sighed, rubbing his sinus. "I feel so stupid."

"Don't. Have you contacted–"

Julian knew what he was going to ask. "Yes. I know you told me the church was good at covering stuff up, but I never…"

"What did they say?"

"They said that they assumed Hell had taken you. They assumed that was the reason to the empty van. They used their power to move the police onto other ventures – their words."

Derek snorted a huff of amusement. It was typical of his experience that those less aware of the supernatural never realise how much authority the church has in concealing conspiracies.

"They've covered up bigger problems before."

Julian sat across from Derek, watching him intently, loosely stirring his coffee with his teaspoon, allowing the ambience of the café to fade into the background and people to walk by unnoticed.

"How does it feel?" Julian asked. "You know, being out of prison?"

Derek smiled into his coffee, giving a slight chuckle.

"Well, I was never really in, was I?" he responded.

"You know what I mean."

Derek sighed, turning his gaze to the window. Julian studied him carefully, wondering what he was thinking. He knew that Derek often liked to philosophise and scrutinise the passing world, contemplating people innocently going about their lives, happily unaware of what dwelled beneath them.

Sometimes, Julian thought, Derek probably envied them. Wished he could have lived his life in ignorance.

"I feel foolish, Julian," Derek finally answered, keeping his gaze focussed on passersby. "That a man of my knowledge and experience could be convinced by such a thing."

"It could have happened to any of us; you can't blame yourself. No one could have predicted something that big taking an entire prison." He took a precarious sip of his coffee. "I certainly didn't."

"Yes, but I should have. Which leads me onto the reason that I believe such a thing was able to happen to me in the first place…"

Derek took in a big, deep breath, holding it for a few seconds, then letting it out. What for, Julian didn't know, but he watched his former mentor intently, awaiting what he was about to say as he took a few moments of mental preparation.

"What do you mean?" Julian prompted.

"That Oscar is a good catch," Derek declared, instantly changing the conversation. "Not only did he manage to take on this entity, he managed to fight his way into a prison of evil, and do it without me, or you, probably never really realising the extent of what he was taking on."

"Yes, he did well."

"Did well? What the boy achieved was remarkable."

"I guess."

Derek smiled.

Julian knew Derek saw a lot of his younger self in him, and this was another moment of familiarity. Julian remembered what Derek was like when they first began his training. Julian was cocky, and Derek was not forthcoming with his praise. It brought him down to earth, but also destroyed his self-belief.

Now, Julian was doing the same thing with Oscar. Maybe it was time to give the praise where it was due.

"You need to watch him," Derek continued. "Harness him. You need to teach him the way."

"Why do you keep saying that *I* need to do this? Surely you're still going to be there? Not hanging up the cross yet, are you?"

Derek sighed. Placed his coffee down. Sat back in his chair and looked deeply upon Julian's face with his ageing eyes.

"I'm dying, Julian."

Julian froze.

"Oh."

47

DEREK LANSDALE HAD BEEN THE BANE OF HELL'S EXISTENCE since his endless tirade began.

The wrath of The Devil fuelled the furious pits of Hell, and the fires lashed out harsher than they ever had. This man... He was the sharp, prickly thorn in his harsh, thick side.

But death was coming for Derek Lansdale.

It was coming slowly, but he wasn't the man he was.

He could not oppose them any longer.

Hell had taken him from the humans, preyed on his guilt and made him weaker day by day.

Four years was enough to destroy him.

Now his illness would do the rest.

But there were more.

The Devil roared a deafening roar at the thought, a scream that pounded through the hot air of the underworld.

The Sensitives.

Heaven's children. Carrying on the battle.

They had to be destroyed.

Not just killed, not just removed – but completely and totally ripped apart and thrown to the flames.

A sinister cackle rang out through the burning amber glow of the underworld.

An idea sparked.

Hell would pick them off one by one.

It was to be so simple.

And they would start with the girl.

April.

Yes.

They would start with her.

WOULD YOU LIKE TWO FREE BOOKS?

Join Rick's Reader's Group for your free and exclusive novella:
www.rickwoodwriter.com/sign-up

CLOSE TO DEATH

RICK WOOD